Balremesh

and other stories

Luther M. Siler

PROSTETNIC
PUBLICATIONS

Dedicated to Myracle, who kept Jayashree alive, and to Gish, who brought Eleazar to life.

Table of Contents

Balremesh and other stories

Foreword

This book is kind of an accident.

My life's been kind of a mess for the last couple of years. I spent a decade and a half as a teacher, a career I was forced out of by sudden-onset, stress-related symptoms at the end of 2016. At one point, just before an ambulance hauled me out of the building, the school nurse told me she'd never seen a *living* human being with a temperature as low as she'd just recorded me having. I resigned from my job at my doctor's orders and started on anti-anxiety meds, also at her orders.

And I barely wrote a damn word of fiction for the next year. My first book came out in 2014. So did my second. My third and fourth came out in 2015. And it is, as I'm writing this, June 25th of 2017 and my fourth book is still "my last book."

That's too long. And I blame the brain meds. They took away my ability to write fiction, which is precisely why I weaned myself off of them a few months ago. Writing is too important to me. Being an author is too important.

Balremesh and other stories is a weird little book. It is, for starters, mostly reprinted material. If you've been following my on my blog at infinitefreetime.com, and *why wouldn't you* follow me at my blog at infinitefreetime.com, since I'm *entertaining as hell*, you may have seen several of these stories before. There are a couple of others that were published elsewhere first and that you may not have seen, though. I have another book coming out, probably sometime in August, that's full of new material.

This one? It's kind of for me, to be honest; a quick side project to convince myself that, yes, I *am* still a damn author and I have words that I have written on my little computery technomagical devices that maybe people might want to read. And I'm releasing it on my 41st birthday, so it's sort of a birthday present to myself. It's cheap; if you're reading this digitally there will never be a circumstance where you spent more than 99 cents for it, and I'm going to give it away for free whenever I can. You might be reading this in print, in which case I promise I sold this to you for as little as I possibly could.

But anyway. Let's talk about the stories a little bit:

Crossroads is the first piece of short fiction Luther M. Siler ever wrote. It's also the shortest in the book that isn't actually a microfiction. It is the direct result of reading two books by Nnedi Okorafor and one by Saladin Ahmed in quick succession.

Confession is set in the same universe as **Crossroads**, but I honestly don't know if it stars the same character. Maybe? I'll let you decide.

Culaqan is the third story in what I'm now thinking of as *The C Trilogy*. It was originally published in L.S. Engler's *World Unknown Review, Vol. 1*, still available at Amazon and no doubt a few other places. There are a bunch of other good stories in there, but this is the only one of them I wrote.

You could be forgiven if you thought that **Nanos Khund and the Traveler** was set in the same world as the C books, but I don't quite think so. Believe it or not, this started off wanting to be a perfectly straightforward superhero story. It ... uh ... didn't end up that way.

The Road to Ramtucko owes its existence to a collaborative writing assignment I threw together at the last moment for one of my 7th grade writing classes. The kids were paired and each was allowed to write for, I don't know, two or three minutes, and then they had to switch and continue the story. No one was allowed to

3

talk. The school librarian and I were paired together as well, so half of this— including the name— was inspired by him. This version of the story is entirely my own work (I've rewritten the entire thing) but you can perhaps tell where he and I were throwing curveballs at each other.

The Disconnected is probably actually the first chapter of a book, and the wonderful thing about being an independent author is that if I want to use it that way someday I can just quietly pull it out of here and no one can stop me. Or I could leave it in! Whee, chaos!

Warrior Jayashree and the Gallows Pole and **Warrior Jayashree and the Young** were actually written in reverse order, despite what the events of the stories might suggest. The first story was written for an H.P. Lovecraft-inspired literary contest (which I did *not* win) and the second was written when a former student threatened to eviscerate me if I didn't give her more Jayashree stories. I know when to do what I'm told.

And then there is **Balremesh**. *Balremesh* was written years before the rest of the stories in this book, and in fact was written before I even knew I would ever publish anything as Luther Siler. (Which is a pen name, if you didn't know that.) It's another Lovecraft-inflected tale, and it's a story that I've come back to over and over and over again throughout the years. I've tried to write a sequel to it, set in the modern day, perhaps half a dozen times and have never been successful. I will manage it eventually.

And toward the end? A bunch of 100-word stories in a section called **Microfictions.** I kinda like 'em. Hopefully you will too.

This Foreword is already longer than at least one of the stories, so I'll stop here and just say this: Thanks, always, for reading, and thanks to those of you who were putting up with me when I wasn't writing and was miserable about it. Your support will be eternally appreciated. Enjoy.

Yours,

Luther M. Siler
Somewhere in Northern Indiana
June 25, 2017

Crossroads

The man sat at the crossroads, legs crossed, his hands at his knees, palms-up, like the Fenidae when they pray. He was dark of skin and eye, his hair falling to his waist in rough braids shot through with grey and festooned with beads and feathers. His beard was tangled, full against his chest, woven through with plaited cords.

He wore a loose robe, gold in color, that had seen rain and sun and dirt and blood.

His face was turned to the morning sun; it should have left him blind. I stood some ways away, observing him. He did not move or speak. He merely waited at the crossroads.

I waited and I watched. The sun rose; the day grew hot. Sweat dripped from my face. The man sat.

Eventually, he spoke. "You may as well come talk with me," he said. "The sun rises high, and you look weary. I have been sitting here for a very long time, and will not be leaving soon."

I adjusted my *khalaat*, testing its edge with my thumb. I did not move, nor did I speak.

The man smiled. "I see that the Nara'ae people are as rude now as when I was a boy. I do not take offense. I ask a second time; come and talk with me. I offer refreshments; food, and drink cool to the parched throat." He gestured with an arm, his first movement since I had seen him. To his right sat a rug, covered in sweetmeats and fruit, with clay wine-jugs, condensation glistening on their sides. The smell of fresh-baked bread reached my nose, and my stomach groaned.

I did not move, nor did I speak. I felt the sun, hot on my face; my armor scorched my shoulders, its weight growing as the day dragged on. My *khalaat* scraped my leg.

The man gestured with his other arm. "I ask a third time; come and talk with me. If my companionship is not to your liking, perhaps others may entice you." To his left was a woman, then another, one dark of eye and skin and the other light. They danced and swayed; the music of the gourd-pipe and the goatskin-drum and the *dzendze* filled the air. Behind them were two young boys, one dark of eye and skin and the other light. The boys sang to the music, and their voices were as those of the spirit-folk.

I did not move, nor did I speak. I felt my heart call out to the dancers, to the singers, *Come away, O! Come away!*

But they heard me not, and they did not come.

The man stood, moving like water. "I ask a final time; come and talk with me." His arms made no movement, and his eyes made no promise. The food and the drink and the women and the boys and the music faded away.

I did not meet his eyes. I strode toward him, and the sun beat down on my face, and my armor was hot upon my shoulders, and my *khalaat* burned my hand as its edge sang through his neck.

I was past the man already as his head rolled from his shoulders and fell to the ground; I never heard his body fall. There was only a whisper, as if a garment had dropped from a height.

I did not look back, to see if the teeth that smiled at me had sharpened points, or if the forehead dry in a sun-maddened day sprouted horns. I walked on, and I turned neither to the right or the left.

For I have lived long, and I know well the creatures that are found at crossroads.

* * *

Confession

"You have killed, have you not?" he asks.

He watches me through heavy-lidded eyes; his tone careful, his face flat. I do not reply. I am not to speak; I am to hear confession. And to judge.

He nods. "I thought so. You have killed. And you have killed many, *yah*? Perhaps more than I have. Perhaps more than old Pakensé ever did. Yet Pakensé is here, and you are there. And Pakensé..."

He trails off, waves his arms at me. He is chained to the wall at the neck and ankles. The ankles, because his arms end in stumps. Old Pakensé has no hands to wave. They have been taken from him.

I do not speak.

"I will tell you a story," Pakensé says. His voice is rough and deep, filled with stones; he has not had anyone to talk to for a long time, but he has screamed. "I will tell you a story, killer-man of the Nara'ae, and then I will say no more. Then you may judge as you wish."

He waits. I sit, cross-legged, my *khalaat* lying bare across my knees. The stone of the floor is cool and damp, and the distance between us too much for his reach.

Pakensé opens his mouth to speak, reconsiders, closes it again. Leans his forehead against the ruined ends of his arms, his eyes closed, as if pondering where to begin. I sit and I wait. I do not speak.

"I want to tell you that I had no choice. And that is true, in some ways. In others, not. When the *ojombwe* began, the men of the towns went from house to house, to find who was with them and who was not. They gave a *khalaat* to each man who said yes. Each man who said no found a mark on his door the next morning. And he did not need to wonder what that mark meant. He soon found himself explaining that he had been drunk on mango wine or taken with a fever; he had not understood. And then he was not given a *khalaat*, but a club."

"The call was given, and we went forth. Each man with his *khalaat*, or his club, with six or eight of his fellows, men he might drink with or fight with on another night. And we hunted. We hunted the Fenidae. And those we found..."

He waits again, pain written on his face.

"They hid, you see. Our coming was no secret; it had been whispered of for weeks, and those who were unbelieving... they could no longer hide. They ran to the woods, to the swamps; they hid under houses and in caves; it was said that some took to the sky itself, but those I did not see. But we were told to return with trophies or not to return at all. And men... men such as we respond poorly to frustration. The Fenidae that we found ... it did not go well for them. The *khalaat's* song was heard from the sun's rise to the moon's."

Pakensé stares at me, his eyes widening only so slightly. This is no confession, not yet; but he is near to one.

I test the edge of my *khalaat*. A single drop of blood falls from my thumb to the stone.

"The *ojombwe* was a week old, and the hunting had grown stale, the few Fenidae who remained too wily to be easily caught. I was with four others when we came upon the altar."

I lift an eyebrow.

"There were three of them, all elders. It should have taken only moments. But suddenly, the other four... they were simply gone, noiseless piles of meat that never could resemble men. Only I was left, and my club fell from my fingers to the ground. The Fenidae had not moved. They prayed, their palms turned to the sky."

Old Pakensé begins to cry.

"I saw it then, killer-man of the Nara'ae. I saw the god of the Fenidae, come down from the heavens and up from the earth. It was radiant of eye, many-limbed, and those eyes foretold naught but pain and blood. A thousand years of hatred and oppression lay plain on its face. And it turned that face toward me."

Pakensé opens his eyes wide for the first time. They are red, redder than heart's blood, a red that should make men blind.

"They told us that the Fenidae were to die because they were blasphemers, killer-man. They told us that their gods were lies and their religion an offense to true gods. But never have I seen our gods. I have been told that they were there. I have prayed to them. But never have I seen them. And that day, I saw the god of the Fenidae, and he was just and terrible. And he... he *spared* me."

He holds up his arms.

"The *ojombworro* found me the next day. There was no blood on my club, and the others... well, I have spoken of them. I had no trophies to deliver to them, nothing to show for our loss. And they lay me on the altar and took my hands. My eyes were as you see now. I see only blood, killer-man."

One breath. Two.

"I know now that the Fenidae held the truth. They held the truth and we yet slaughtered them like cattle, like rabbits in a cage. But we did not slaughter their god, killer-man, and I have beheld the face of that god and felt his anger. He waits; I know not the reason. But he will come for me. He comes for all of us. And the song of your *khalaat* no longer brings me fear. If confession you seek, you have it. Do what you must."

Old Pakensé falls to his knees, his head down; he speaks no more. He shall never speak again, I think, not if I leave him to sit by his wall until time turns his chains to dust; not if I unlock his chains and let him leave this place, his choices once again his own. Or my *khalaat's* song may end his life; his song shall be heard no longer regardless.

I rise from the floor.

He does not move.

And I pass my judgment.

*　*　*

Culaqan

He paces outside for an hour before mustering the courage to even approach my door. He believes that he is hidden, far from my home and among the trees, but my vision extends farther than he knows. He begins to approach three times, turning away twice and retreating to his hide. When he knocks, he is all chest; puffed and preening like a bird, his mainhand never far from the *khalaat* at his waist.

I do not let him in at first. He knocks, timidly, then controls his fear and pounds on my door. I suspect he may have damaged the finish; the dallo tree's wood is soft and bruises easily. He has made me wait. I return the favor. I watch him through the door, waiting for the confidence to bleed away, for the swollen chest and erect shoulders to droop a bit.

Only when he turns away do I allow the door to open. It opens slowly, and it *creeeeeaks*. He freezes, turns. He cannot see inside; I have chosen to deny that from him. He touches the *khalaat* again, reassuring himself, and enters. I am seated on the floor, reclining against a pillow, food and drink scattered on small plates around me. I let the smell of warm bread and honey enter his nostrils.

His eyes devour me, traveling over my form. For this visitor, I have made myself younger, more supple. He would like what he sees, were he not so afraid. I meet his gaze without blinking and he almost trembles. He touches the sword yet again, his fingers drifting over the hilt like the caress of an uncertain lover. I gesture at the food, but he makes no move to sit. Nor does he speak.

I give him two minutes. He stands in silence, awkward. It occurs to me how terribly young he is; the Nara'ae have sent him to me because he is the least among them. I think I will ignore the insult.

"You were not sent to me to gawk, child."

He blinks. *Child* is not a name he has been called in some time, despite his youth. Opens his mouth, closes it again.

"Perhaps you could tell me why you are here."

"There is ..."

He hesitates again. Masters himself, hopefully for the last time.

"There is a dragon. The Nara'ae ... *request* the assistance of your ... people."

"And who are *my* people, young Nara'ae?"

"The Culaqan witches, madam."

He has chosen well, and named us properly; the Nara'ae have called us by less polite names in the past. I nod.

"Tell me of this dragon."

He takes a deep breath; this speech is memorized, and not without some difficulty, I expect.

"A *kilikeen*-- a spotted dragon-- has been reported raiding the villages near here. At first it was only taking livestock; scattered sheep and goats and pigs, nothing so large as cattle. Men were sent for it; a week of weeks have passed and they have not returned."

"Who has seen this spotted dragon?"

"None who have lived."

"Then how do we know it is a dragon? And not, perhaps, a hungry outcast, or even a pack of wolves? Livestock can be lost for many reasons. Men, even more."

"There has been spoor," he responds. "Footprints. Dung. And these." He reaches into a pouch at his belt and pulls out a handful of scales. Most are a creamy white in color; some are a deeper brown, and larger. All are much too big for any ordinary lizard.

I take them from him and set them aside. I have seen the scales of these dragons before, many times.

"How many legs does this dragon have?"

"I ... I do not know, madam."

"You would not, not without having seen it," I respond. "And you did not lie." Spotted dragons had been seen with dozens of legs; six to twelve were more common.

"I was told to utter no untruth."

"You follow orders well. But I am confused; I have not known the Nara'ae to give up after only one sending of a war party. An unsuccessful outing is usually followed by a larger, more experienced one. And I have heard naught of this dragon from other sources. Why approach my people now? What keeps you from killing it yourself?"

"We believe it has killed a family," he said. "The last raid was larger. Instead of one or two animals taken it was a dozen or more. And the home full with blood, and things that were no longer people."

I inhale through my teeth. *Killed a family.* "More than one of the beasts, then?"

"Or it has shed, or is about to," he responded. "Which makes it trebly dangerous as before. We ask you to accompany a war party. We do not seek to throw away lives unnecessarily, ours *or* yours."

I nod.

"And, to be clear, because you have not said the words yet: you wish me to kill this *kilikeen* for you?" I know the answer. Killing is always the way for the Nara'ae. Always.

Regardless, he bristles at the suggestion. "We wish for you to assist as you may. Nothing more. The Nara'ae do not need anything done *for* them."

I smile.

"When are we to begin?"

"Now, madam. If, that is, you agree."

I do.

*   *   *

I allow myself one hour to collect supplies for the trip. I own little; when I am done there is not much left in my home, and less still that I would be troubled by never seeing again. It has been a very long time since the Nara'ae sought the help of the Culaqan, and it has not been long since they hunted us as they hunt the spotted dragons. The boy watches as I close the door, and continues to watch as I shake a seed-pod from a gorrah-tree over the jambs, the lintel, the sill and the latch. I mumble to myself as I do so; he will believe I have laid a strong magic on my home. I have not, but the seeds are small and sticky and if they have been disturbed, I will see it if I return. Fear is often just as potent as magic.

He does not speak as I join him, turning on one heel

and walking off. He appears to hope that his long legs will carry him ahead of me; I have run faster men than he into exhaustion. He is winded in an hour and slows down; I offer to lift him on my shoulders and am coldly rebuffed. *I like this boy*, I think, *but he takes himself too seriously.*

In three hours, he suggests pausing for food. I remember the honey and the bread I offered him earlier, and shrug my shoulders. I do not need to eat very often any longer. He sits cross-legged on the side of the road, in the shade of a shirra-tree, and pulls a knife and some fruit from a bag. He offers me some; I decline.

In no time, the *shirrus* is on him. It is young, only five to six feet long and probably not very venomous yet. And it misses him with its first bite, and does not pin his arms to his sides with its many legs. No adult *shirrus* would make these mistakes; they kill in moments, often before the victim is aware they are in danger.

To his credit, he does not panic. He rolls forward, the *shirrus* tumbling from his shoulders, and comes to his feet with his *khalaat* in one hand and a short knife in the other. The *shirrus* recognizes that it has lost the chance at surprise and attempts to scurry up its tree again. His *khalaat* ends the beast's song before it makes it halfway back to the branches.

He breathes heavily, more from surprise than strain or exhaustion. I look; he is scratched, but not bitten.

"You knew that the beast was in the tree," he says.

"I knew that was a shirra-tree," I say. "But you sat underneath it so quickly, with no thought for the consequences. I thought you believed the tree unoccupied." I pull down a branch, pulling off some leaves and showing him their telltale serrated shape and green-to-red coloration. The *shirrus* lives only in these trees. There is rarely more than one at a time, however.

"We should burn the tree," I say. They are rarely seen this close to civilized places; perhaps it *has* been unoccupied for some time. He nods, but does not speak. We pile loose leaves and branches under the tree and I ignite it with a word. I also send a spark from a striking-stone I have hidden in my hand into the driest of the leaves. He does not see; he does not expect to.

They are so easily fooled, the Nara'ae.

In time, we reach the outskirts of a village.

"I thought we were to hunt this *kitikeen*, not to wait for it," I say.

"I was told to bring you to the Nara'ae first," he says. "And it was thought that you might wish to see the results of the last attack. It happened in this very village."

"Show me," I say.

*   *   *

The Nara'ae are correct; this destruction can be from nothing but a dragon, and a dragon entering molt, at that. There are cast-off browned scales everywhere, and tracks, and the few body parts large enough to search for wounds bear the marks of four-clawed feet and teeth of the right size and shape. The *kilikeen* go into feeding frenzy before molt; they eat until eating more would kill them, then fall into a kind of sleep while their bodies shed their skins. A freshly-shed *kilikeen* is the purest white, with spots of brown; the brown patches grow and the scales grow larger as the beast gets closer to a new molt. Sometimes, after a molt, the *kilikeen* will have grown a new pair of legs. The frenzies for these molts are especially destructive.

Our *kilikeen* may have been growing two or three new pairs of legs under its old skin, judging from the severity of this destruction.

"Take me to your clansmen," I tell the boy.

He nods quickly and strides off again. They are in the fields, pawing through the remains of the livestock the *kilikeen* has left behind. Four; not a full warband, even with the boy there. They do not introduce themselves and I do not ask their names. It is clear to them what I am; it is clear to me what they are. That will be enough.

"Do you know where she has gone?" I ask.

The eldest among them carries a spear, not a *khalaat*. He points toward the east. "It has left a trail that even this boy could follow with his eyes closed. There are leavings from its meal and it has left its blazes on the trees it has passed as well. We have sent some on ahead to discover its den and return to us. They were told to avoid the beast if they encounter it, not to attempt an attack."

He blinks, as if reconsidering what he has heard. "She? You know that it is female?"

"There are signs, for those who know how to see. Are there so few of you?" I ask. "The boy led me to believe there were many warbands here."

The Nara'ae shakes his head, disgusted. "The blood of my ancestors runs weak in this part of the world. We were three warbands strong yesterday. Many have left for their homes. The beast's ... *message* has unmanned them."

I feign a gasp; he will know it for the insult it is. To my people joining the Nara'ae is itself an unmanning. But I will not provoke him more than necessary. They will find this *kilikeen* for me; if it eats a few of them along the way that is no loss, so long as one of them returns to guide the rest of us. I have some spells of location, but they work poorly for things I have never myself encountered, and I am certain that I have not seen this *kilikeen* before.

"Do we wait, then?" I ask. "Or do we follow?"

"We have waited already," the man responds. "But you have arrived. There is no further reason to remain. Unless you have your own preparations to make."

I make a show of examining the site, drawing lines on my face and arms with the blood of the *kilikeen's* kills, some of which has not yet fully soaked into the ground, and murmuring words in a voice too low for the men to understand. There is no need for any of it; I know what I need to know and have seen all I care to. But it is best for these men to believe otherwise. I continue until they shift their feet and suck at their teeth with impatience, and then I toss some of the blood into the air with some leaves and grass and dirt and watch how the wind blows it back to the ground. The wind blows them to the east, just as it always does.

"Your trackers are correct," I say to him. "We may proceed."

*   *   *

The elder is right; a child could follow this trail. The *kilikeen* is either surprisingly large or has grown very clumsy in the latter stages of molt; the ground cover is trampled flat in a trail four feet wide and larger plants are broken or hurled out of the way. The path is straight east, away from the places of men and into the wilderness, where high trees give shelter from the heat of the day. We walk for an hour, eventually encountering the rest of their war band. There are three men left, bringing their group to nine. These men are younger and do not look blooded. I grin despite my caution. These elders have sent their young on the hazardous journeys; one to find me and the others to find the dragon, and remained behind themselves to "investigate" in safety. *Unmanned, indeed*, I think.

They clasp hands and posture and discuss for a few

minutes; I wander on ahead a bit, trying to determine how much farther we have to travel. If we get too close, she will hear us coming; her vision extends far, and her hearing farther.

They send the boy to speak with me. "Two miles, they say. They want to know how you plan to help."

"They will see that when I see their dragon," I tell him. "If there are two more miles to cover, then we should cover them. They do not want to face a *kilikeen* in full molt after darkness falls." I stride off; let them try to catch up with me for a while.

The sun is just beginning to set as we encounter the *kilikeen's* cave. The entrance is littered with spoor; remains of her meals, more scales, and large piles of loose branches and screen that she has dragged over to attempt to camouflage her lair from the outside. She is close to molt indeed, if she is trying to hide underground. The men move some of the branches out of the way; the darkness inside the cave is near total.

The elder stomps forward, making a racket the *kilikeen* could hear in her sleep. "There are eight of us. Less than a full warband, and we have sent a full warband against this animal before. Your magic is said to be powerful. You will bring the spotted dragon from its den and we will all destroy it."

I shake my head.

"You are foolish, old one. She is hiding; you can see that. This means that we are in luck; she may be in molt right now, which means she will be sluggish and easy to capture. I will lay a magic upon your men that will allow you to see in her darkness and give strength to your limbs and speed to your legs and sturdiness to your skin. I will lay a second magic upon your *khalaats*, that they may cleave her skin as an axe cleaves dallo wood. She will fall to you like wheat to a scythe."

He nods.

"Give me your *khalaats*," I say. "I must begin quickly."

*   *   *

The spells are long, and complicated, and involve burning of plants that I send them to find and bring to me, and I nod sagely when they bring me the wrong ones and burn them anyway. I dance and chant and hurl spices and sprinkle things upon them from jars that I have brought with me. By the time I am finished the boy looks excited enough to fight the *kilikeen* himself and even the older men are puffed and walking with their chests again. Their *khalaats* are stained with tomato juice and coriander and have had words half-remembered from children's songs mumbled over them. My hands have been waved and my fingers twisted into uncomfortable positions.

They are ready to fight the dragon, these Nara'ae; as ready as ever they can be. The elder, true to his nature, sends the six youngest in, including the boy.

"Enter quietly," I tell them. "You will have an easier time of it if she does not hear you coming. Strike quickly and with determination; you will succeed. Bring me the teeth; they are useful in my spells."

They nod, draw their swords, and enter the cave.

Some little time later, there are screams.

And they do not come out.

*   *   *

He is angry, the elder, so very angry. And he knows fear, perhaps more fear than he has ever known in his life. He shoves his spear in my face and shrieks at me in a language that even I do not understand; perhaps the Nara'ae have their own that is not taught to outsiders. His partner stands uncertainly at the edge of the clearing before the cave; he is torn between helping his friend and fleeing.

I do not speak; I stare at the elder's eyes. I make myself younger and more innocent in them. *This* is true magic, you see; there are no words, no gestures, no special ingredients to burn or eat or throw. True magic can be effected by merest desire for it. But they do not know that, and they would not believe it if they did.

"You. *You* will destroy this beast," he says, shaking the spear. "You will destroy it *now*, Culaqan witch. You will destroy it, or *I* will destroy *you*."

He makes no move to help, or to follow me into the cave.

"You may try," I say. "You are not guaranteed success, but you may try. But I will see to this dragon for you nonetheless. She will cause you but a little more trouble."

I cast no spells on my own person; no chanting of words or waving of hands, no burning of plants that foolish people think are magic. I turn and walk into the cave.

The cave is deep, and dark. I encounter the six quickly enough; they are torn roughly, and burned. Killed without consideration for eating. *She IS ready to molt*, I think. These meals are for later.

The dragon is in the back of the cave, lying on her side, breathing heavily. She raises her head when I enter. She is eight-legged now, but I can see the new ones writhing under the old skin, which is almost entirely brown, her spots obliterated; she will be large indeed when she reaches her full growth.

She inhales, sharply. I raise a hand. Light fills the cave, and she pauses.

I know what you are, sister, I tell her.

She glares at me, balefully, eyes full of malice, but does not attack.

You are no killer.

Her eyes tell me otherwise; her eyes are full with killing, and eating, and destruction.

Let me help you.

Her head collapses back down to the ground, her energy spent. I must work quickly; if she molts, she will be uncontrollable again for a while, and I do not wish to battle an uncontrolled twelve-legged *kilikeen*.

I place my hands on her smooth head, next to her eyes, and concentrate. True magic fills the cave, and a mighty roaring fills my ears, and then a moment of pure silence and darkness.

*   *   *

I do not know how much the elder hears, but he and his clansman are still there, unnerved but resolute, when I emerge from the cave, the girl on my arm. She is naked, bloody; I call to him for a blanket, a covering of some kind, and he produces one from a pack.

"She was captured?" he asks. I do not answer; he may think what he wishes.

"And the dragon?"

"What is left of it is inside," I say. "You may take what you wish of the spoils. I have what I need." I speak truth; it is almost the dragon's entire body that has been shed, not merely the skin, and it has been left behind. She is Culaqan now, no longer *kilikeen*, and it looks as if I shall be returning to my home again after all.

There is a new witch to raise.

Nanos Khund and the Traveler

The boy played in the dust at the side of the road, the noonday sun beating down on shaved head and bare back. He looked but a tenyear in age, and his scrawny frame and long teeth spoke of poor nutrition and hard living.

He heard something approaching in the distance. His head perked up, his ball and stick forgotten. What was that sound? *A horse*, he thought. Surely it could not be such. He had heard that men rode horseback, far away, and once a traveling witch had used a horse skull as her tema, but he had never seen a living one, and certainly not one bearing a rider.

The road curved away from him, his view blocked by a copse of trees. He considered running to meet the rider and did not, then considered hiding from the rider and did not do that either.

The horse rounded the curve and his breath caught in his throat. His knees locked, and he thought again to run. This time he wished to move, but could not. The horse was huge, towering above him. The man riding the horse was even larger, a great hammer upon his back, five feet long if it was an inch. He wore a helm set atop a snarl of red curls that grew into a long beard, and armor made of plaited leather. His skin was shockingly pale. A brace of spears was strapped to the horse's side, their points gleaming in the daylight.

"Boy," the rider said. It was more of a command than a greeting.

The boy nodded, too frightened to speak. How did the man not burn like dry grass in the noonday sun? And such hair! He had never seen the like. When his was allowed to grow, it would come in black, as did everyone else's he knew. And that hammer! He had seen warriors—his own brother had joined the Muhanguilat just a few years ago—but he had seen no one go to battle with a warhammer. From the look of the thing, it was well-used. The rider was certainly large enough to wield it.

"Your village. It is nearby, yes? How far?" His voice was startlingly high, given his frame. For an insane moment, the boy wanted to laugh, then reconsidered. He pointed down the road, trying to prevent his arm from shaking.

"Not far, then," the man said. The boy nodded again

"I have come to kill a certain man," he said. "I will hazard a guess: that you know who this man is, and how to find him."

The boy's posture altered instantly. His eyes brightened, a spark of what might have been hope. He straightened to his full height, meeting the man's gaze fully for the first time.

"Nanos Khund," he said. "You come to kill Nanos Khund."

The man considered this for a moment, then laughed.

"I do," he said. "I come to kill, as you say, *Nanos Khund*. And you? You will help me, won't you."

The boy nodded.

"I will," he said.

*   *   *

The visitor known as Nanos Khund had arrived nearly two years ago, during the rainy season, before the grass and the trees turned to dust. He had worn clothing of strange make, a blue as bright as the sky, tight to his body and as shiny as polished quartz. He wore a black helm, a strange clear material covering his eyes, and wore a cloak that hung down to his ankles. At first, the men had laughed. Only women expecting a child would wear such a cloak.

Nanos Khund had pointed at the first man to laugh, and a blue light filled the air. The man collapsed, his body shriveled and ancient. After that, no one laughed when Nanos Khund was near. He killed four more, two elders and two strong warriors, before the rest of the village bent the knee to him. A brace of the Muhanguilat arrived the next week, notified of the intruder by someone, the boy knew not who. Nanos Khund took control of their minds and set them to building a high walled tower for him in the center of the village, larger and grander by far than anything else for weeks' ride in any direction, and made of strange stone, produced during the dark of night and worked by unknown hands.

When Nanos Khund's home was finished, the Muhanguilat stood upon its walls facing the sun and killed themselves as one. Their bodies remained upon the walls, as none had dared to suggest that Nanos Khund allow them to be moved.

Three days later, the laughter and the screams had begun. They went on for four days, echoing from Nanos Khund's tower, maniacal and insane. The boy remembered being huddled with his family in their home, not daring to leave, for who knew what devilry Nanos

Khund worked in the night? Who knew what had possessed him, a man already controlling more power than any of them had ever witnessed?

No; they hid. They hid and they prayed, and they hoped that Nanos Khund would disappear as abruptly as he had arrived. And, in a way, he did.

On the fifth day, Nanos Khund emerged from his tower, his strange clothes shredded, the marks of his own fingernails scored deep into the flesh of his face. His helm was gone, as was his cloak. The boy had watched him through the crack in a barely-opened front door as he entered a neighbor's home and emerged, noiselessly, wearing the neighbor's clothing. Since then, he mostly remained in his tower. The villagers brought him food and drink and new raiment, leaving it by the open gate to his home, but never crossing the threshold. Once they had forgotten, or perhaps someone had resolved to serve Nanos Khund no longer.

The next day, four villagers did not wake up from their sleep, or perhaps they slept decades in a night, for their bodies were impossibly aged, from healthy and strong to infirm ancients overnight. One had been an infant, still in its cradle. They had had to destroy the cradle to remove the body, now much too large and gruesomely crowded into the space.

No one neglected Nanos Khund's needs again. In fact, they had increased their tribute, occasionally leaving live animals or tools with his food and garments. The stories of him spread, and none came to the boy's village to trade, or to bargain for a wife or a husband, any longer.

Until the man on the horse.

*   *   *

"What is your name?" the man asked. "I cannot very well call you *boy* forever."

"Edo is my youthname," the boy replied. "I do not know my life's name yet, and I could not share it with you if I did."

"Edo," the man said, as if the sounds were unfamiliar. He looked at him, waiting for something.

The boy did not speak.

"You are not going to ask my name? So be it. I will tell you anyway. It is..." and he made a sound, deep in his throat, like the crashing of a tree blown down during a storm.

The boy started, and forgot courtesy. "That is not a name!"

The man raised an eyebrow. "Are you certain?" And then he made the sound again. The boy listened carefully. There were sounds in that name he had never heard, sounds he was certain his mouth and tongue could never make. He shook his head.

"Fascinating," the man said, and thought deeply for a moment. "What is it called, in your tongue, when water falls like a rock from the air, and along with it the air roars, and bright light flashes in streaks across the sky, but does not touch the ground?"

But you are speaking my tongue, Edo thought, but did not say. And then he was startled again, as he thought more about what the man had said.

"We have no word for such a thing," he said. "Water does fall from the sky, but I have never seen it ... *rocky*. We call the roaring thunder, and the bright light is called lightning, but it is called lightning whether it strikes the ground or not. The water is called rain, or a storm, depending on how much of it is falling."

For several seconds, the man did not speak again.

"What do you call a man who stays outdoors during such an event, and takes control of it, and breaks its will with his own might? What do you call the man who controls the water from the sky?"

The boy laughed. "That would be no man, but a woman. We have stories of the sky-goddess. Her name is Ratheme."

"You will call me Ratheme, then," said the man.

The boy laughed, forgetting courtesy again. "But that is a woman's name!"

"I have been called worse," the man said. "Ratheme it is. It is close enough, for what I must do."

"Nanos Khund is very dangerous," Edo said. "How will you kill him?"

"I will need to consider that very carefully," Ratheme said. "Let me know when we are close to your village, but before it can be seen. You will need to describe it to me with the greatest precision, before Nanos Khund knows I am near."

"I will," Edo said. "We are not far now."

"Then we should stop," Ratheme said, stopping his horse. "I will find myself shelter near here. You return home, and come back with food. I have not paused to eat in some time, and my stomach grows impatient."

"I will," Edo said again, turning to run to home.

"Do not be seen, boy," Ratheme said. "And speak to no one of me. Nanos Khund's hearing may be sharper than we think."

*   *   *

It was dark before Edo returned. Ratheme had created a shelter, and Edo only recognized it as such because he knew the land so well, for there was a low hill where there had been no hill before. Edo stood before it, confused, wondering to himself what he should do. As he watched, a gap opened in the side of the hill. A light shone from inside, lighting Ratheme's silhouette from behind. Ratheme beckoned to Edo. The interior of the space was bare, the walls radiating light on their own. Two cushions lay on the floor.

Edo stopped at the entrance, his fascination warring with his fear.

"Is it magic?" he asked. He touched the outside of the

hill. It felt like soil and grass, but surely there had been no time for anything to grow!

"It may as well be," Ratheme said. "Please, come inside. I do not want anyone to see you. And I can already smell the food you have brought."

Edo came bearing roasted goat seasoned with makimurri and wrapped in gorra leaves. Ratheme was right; the meal smelled delicious, and he had struggled to avoid eating any of it while returning to the stranger. Ratheme offered him a piece and devoured the rest in short order.

"Tell me of Nanos Khund," he said. "All that you can."

"He lives in his tower, and rarely comes out," the boy said. "I have never been inside. We provide him with his food and water, and sometimes tools and clothes. He has not exited since... since the last deaths." A tear slid down a cheek.

"You saw them," Ratheme said.

"I was told," he said. "My parents would not let me see them. They were... they were *old*. Ancient. As if they had lived a lifetime overnight."

Ratheme nodded.

"This was how long ago?"

"Not very long after he arrived," Edo said. "And since then I have not seen him. We have only heard him."

"Are you certain he remains in the tower?"

"There are screams sometimes, and laughter. Lights,

but not from flame. I have not seen him. He sees us. And the supplies always disappear, during the night."

Ratheme nodded again, thinking deeply.

"I shall do this in the morning," he said. "And I shall do it where all of you can see me. You deserve to witness this scourge being removed."

The boy smiled broadly, then looked around.

"I... uh... I do not know how to leave," he said.

Ratheme gestured, and the gap reopened.

"You will hear from me after the sun rises," he said.

Edo smiled again, and ducked outside. Ratheme sat and listened to the sound of bare feet on dirt as the boy ran back to his home.

*   *   *

Edo was awake well before sunrise, and sat on the threshold of his home, waiting for something to happen. It was strangely cold, even for the early morning just before the rainy season, and his skin prickled in the breeze.

Slowly the sun rose, and Ratheme did not appear. The sunlight was curious; it brought no warmth with it, and Edo saw the world as if through a haze of yellow. The air itself somehow looked sickly and weak. Nanos Khund's tower loomed overhead, its shadow falling over what had once been a thriving marketplace.

Ratheme did not appear.

Edo watched. The sun continued to rise.

And from a cloudless sky, three bolts of lightning struck the parapet of the tower.

The light blinded Edo, and the physical force behind the sound flung him to the ground like a child's toy. He screamed, covering his eyes, only barely aware of others around him doing the same.

When he regained his vision, Ratheme stood in front of the tower. His helm was silver now, a silver that shone even in the weak light, and carried his hammer one-handed. He wore his spears upon his broad back.

He raised the hammer over his head, and the thunder roared, and the sky darkened, but no clouds passed overhead. Edo blinked, wondering if he was going blind again. Had Ratheme's power weakened the *sun itself?* This red-maned stranger was no mere warrior.

"You shall come out," Ratheme shouted, and his voice was like a god's. "You shall come out, or I shall tear this place down around you." He spun the hammer once over his head, and set its haft into the ground at his feet.

"Nanos Khund! You have one minute. Choose!"

Edo looked around, wondering where his neighbors were. He saw no one, but there was furtive movement behind windows. His people were all watching, but none wished to be seen doing so. He remained at the threshold, part of him wondering if his parents would dare to try and force him inside.

The air filled with manic laughter, the laughter of one

who laughs to keep from screaming. The gates to Nanos Khund's tower swung open. And Nanos Khund himself stepped out.

THAT is Nanos Khund? Edo thought. The creature who emerged from the tower gates bore little resemblance to the dangerous killer he had feared for so long. He looked frail, malnourished, his hair thinning and his teeth and fingernails ungroomed. His clothes, once the finest available in the village, were in rags that hung loosely on his body.

If he had wandered into the village today, he would not have been an object of fear. He would have been offered charity.

Nanos Khund laughed again, a sound on the edge of pure hysteria.

"You? It cannot be. My isolation has affected my mind. That *cannot be you*."

And then he made the sound again, the sound that had come from Ratheme's throat when he had told Edo his name.

"I am called Ratheme here," Ratheme said. "The translator cannot cope with the name you know me by."

"Ratheme," Nanos Khund said. He tilted his head to the side. "*Ratheme*. Their goddess of the air, no? Close enough, I suppose."

Ratheme lifted his hammer from the ground, balancing its weight on his shoulder.

"You know how this ends, do you not, Nanos Khund?"

He laughed again. "At least call me by my proper name. None of these fools were ever able to say it."

"*Doctor Nanosecond*, then," Ratheme said. "It took a while to find you, when last you escaped us. Intelligentsia and the One were actually *working together*. And then your apprentice brought us the ruins of your time machine."

"Decade betrayed me, did he?" Nanos Khund said. "No surprise. He was always weak and foolish. But I must admit, old friend: I do *not* know how this ends. Did the Arbiters actually send you to arrest me? My Timeship exploded when I came here. Nothing in this era will ever allow me to repair it. And the rest of my equipment ran out of charge months ago."

He looked up, addressing everything else to the village.

"Do you hear that, fools? I have been as harmless as a kitten since the last four I killed. And you continued to fear me *anyway*. The weakest child in the village could have defeated me before the last rainy season came."

He turned his gaze back to Ratheme.

"And here you are, weather-master, to... what? To call me to account for my crimes? To return me to our time? Nothing could please me more." He put his wrists together, extending his arms to Ratheme.

"Arrest me. Take me home. Remove me from this place and from this time. I hate it here. I have *always* hated it here."

"I promised to kill you," Ratheme said, and his hammer began to crackle with energy. "Not to bring you home."

Nanos Khund, for the first time, looked frightened. "You cannot."

"I can," Ratheme said. "Your final crime, before you disappeared. Do you happen to recall it?"

"A robbery," Nanos Khund said. "A simple robbery. Most of the funds I stole weren't even *real*. The money was..." and then another rush of sounds, unintelligible to Edo.

"You killed a guard on your way into the building," Ratheme said. "One. One *only*. But that guard was one of mine."

"A worshipper?" Nanos Khund said. "Your cult has been dead for generations."

"More than that," Ratheme said. "You are right. The Arbiters sent me to bring you back. They will not be terribly disappointed when they discover that I was unable to." He pointed his hammer at Nanos Khund, and a profusion of lightning shot from the head, lifting the man into the air and flinging him back into his own courtyard. Ratheme followed. Edo looked around, noticing that some of his neighbors were beginning to emerge from their homes to watch the battle. There was another flash of energy and a scream from within the courtyard. Edo jumped to his feet and ran, eager to watch Nanos Khund die.

———

He saw Nanos Khund standing over Ratheme, blue energy firing from his hands into Ratheme's chest, as the red-haired warrior aged before Edo's eyes.

"No," the boy whispered.

"Idiot," Nanos Khund growled. "I tell you my tools are depowered and you fire *lightning* at me? The Arbiters chose the wrong hero. They should have sent Feral. He never hesitated to kill. You should have taken my *head* off with that hammer. And now you're going to die."

He looked up at Edo and the rest of the villagers, some of whom stood behind him.

"And after I'm finished with him..." he said. "All of you. *All* of you. No one lives this time. If this pathetic hamlet is not worth ruling, *Doctor Nanosecond will destroy it and find another.*"

Edo looked around, panicking. Ratheme's hammer was on the ground, but he and Nanos Khund were between him and it and it was too heavy to lift anyway. There was nothing. There was—

Spears. Ratheme's spears had been knocked from his back, and was only a few paces away.

The boy moved as quickly as ever he had before. This had to be done *now*. He ran toward the spears, snatching one from the ground at a dead run, and charged Nanos Khund.

The villain did not notice him coming until it was too late. Khund raised a hand, and Edo felt terrible pain as the blue energy washed over him. Then the tip of the spear pierced Nanos Khund in the throat, and he collapsed, dead instantly.

Edo fell over the body, panting heavily, recovering from the pain. He pushed himself up from the ground.

Something was wrong. He looked at his arms. They were *larger*. Muscled, sheened with sweat. He ran a hand over his head. He had *hair*. It hung past his shoulders, satin-black and straight.

He looked at himself. Nanos Khund's aging fire had touched him only for a moment. It had not had time to kill him. It had brought him to his *majority*.

A cough brought him back to himself, and back to Ratheme. The warrior—but what was he, truly?—lay on the ground, aged to unrecognizability.

Edo ran to his side, dropping to a knee behind him.

"Hammer," the old man whispered. Edo looked for it, lifting the huge weapon easily and bringing it to the dying man.

Ratheme clasped his hand over Edo's, his grip surprisingly strong. "Yours now," he coughed. "The hammer, and the responsibility that comes with it. The winds, the lightning, the thunder, the rain and the snow. All yours now. Yours to control."

His eyes rolled up into his head, the whites exposed, and he began mumbling in a language that Edo did not know. Edo *felt* the hammer attune itself to him. His awareness expanded to take in all that was around him, and he washed the darkness from the air, bringing back the sunlight that Ratheme had held back.

"You said you did not know your life's name," Ratheme said. "Do you know it now?"

Edo concentrated, and a word entered his mind. He could not say it—not yet—but he knew that it was his destiny, and that he would soon enough.

"Say goodbye to your family," Ratheme said. "The horse will take you back. You have to let the Arbiters know what happened here. *You* are *me* now, boy. Be better at it than I was."

Edo blinked away tears as Ratheme took a final breath, then lay still.

He stood up, balancing his hammer on one shoulder.

He kicked Nanos Khund's dead body, and was amazed at how far it flew. The raw strength in this new body was astounding.

"Tear the tower down," he said to the crowd, and went to find his horse.

*   *   *

Luther M. Siler

The Road to Ramtucko

It was already the wrong kind of night to be outside— driving snow, sleet, and just enough moonlight to light up the fog but not enough to see by. To make things worse, the damn horse had just thrown a shoe, and it was showing no interest at all in doing any more carrying of *people* tonight. It stood still, one leg held off the ground, steam pouring off its sides, chuffing and panting steadily.

Eleazar Gishovski hated horses. He'd heard there were people working on inventing some sort of mechanical cart that cut the beast out of the picture altogether; he'd never seen one and half figured they were just a rumor the world had cobbled together to mock him. But it was ride the horse or walk, and he had to be in Ramtucko by morning—hell, he had to be there by *yesterday* morning—and that meant riding, no choice. He'd been summoned; there was plague in Ramtucko, and his skills were needed. He'd borrowed the horse from a friend. Allan would kill him if he'd lamed the horse, if the plague didn't get him first.

He slid off the horse's back gingerly, hoping he'd be able to figure out how to get back on without someone to boost him. He looked at the horse, then looked at its hoof.

"I'm just going to look and see if there's a rock in there or something," he said. The shoe was definitely gone, but maybe there was something else wrong. "Don't hurt me. I'm trying to be nice." *Horses don't eat people, do they?* he thought.

There was not a rock stuck in the horse's hoof.

There was a *diamond* stuck in the horse's hoof. And a bloody great big one at that.

What the hell was *that* doing there? Something nagged at the back of his head, an uneasy feeling quite out of sync with just having found a diamond, but he pushed it away. How did he get it out? Pry it? With what? He had a penknife and his bag with his surgical tools, but he wasn't sure the horse was going to sit still while he sawed away at its foot. Leaving it there wasn't an option; it was obviously hurting the horse even above and beyond having lost the shoe, but he needed a way to get it out without getting kicked in the head. The damn horse was *named* Kicker, for God's sake; Allan had said it like it was a joke but Eleazar wasn't interested in finding out the hard way that he was wrong.

The damn diamond was *huge*.

He felt around in his pockets until he found his penknife. "Just gonna pry this out," he said to Kicker. "Might hurt for a second. You'll be fine." He tried to project feelings of *soothing* and *gentle* and *please don't kick me in my face* to the horse, who glared at him as if contemplating abandoning its natural vegetarianism.

He gripped the horse's hoof and carefully levered his knife under the edge of the diamond. He pried, carefully.

There was a very loud *boom*. Eleazar had enough time to think the phrase *horses don't go boom* and then the horse charged off, galloping awkwardly on three legs. The diamond was nowhere to be seen. *Did I get it? Was it out of the hoof?*

He had no idea.

What he did know was that the horse was apparently no longer concerned about its hoof, as it abruptly wheeled back around, regaining its usual four-footed gait and charging directly at him. He had time to think *DIVE!* but no time to actually do it; the horse bowled him over, sending him flying, and charged off into the night, Eleazar's bag and all his gear with it.

He lay on the ground in a stupor for a moment, trying to shake the clouds out of his head and hoping nothing was broken. All he knew was that everything hurt; he'd never been run over by a horse before and had no interest in ever repeating the experience. He shook his head and opened his eyes.

Something glittered in the snow, not two yards from his face. It kept swimming in and out of focus, along with the rest of the world. *The diamond?* He reached for it, hoping against hope.

It was the missing horseshoe.

"Useless," he muttered, and hurled the shoe into the woods. There was no way he was shoeing an angry, fast-moving horse that wanted nothing to do with him even before he magically found the nails and hammer that he'd need. If that was even what you needed to shoe horses. It was worse than useless to him– and the horse was *gone*. There was nothing to do but to either try and find the diamond (which, for all he knew, was still attached to the horse) or head for town on foot.

Oh, wait, he thought. There had been a boom. What in the world had the boom been for?

There was a second boom.

This one was *much* closer to him; he saw trees shake a few dozen yards away and heard at least a few fall to the ground.

Run, he thought, and did. No time to look for the diamond. If it was there at all, it would still be there later.

He stumbled to his feet and took off pell-mell down

the path, tripping a few times and nearly losing his footing. All around him, debris—rocks, dirt, branches—was hitting the ground and flying through the air. Something caught him in the chest, tossing him flat on his back. A wire, strung between trees. No, not really a wire—more of a *cable*. Strung like a tripwire. At chest height, where no human being not bent on running for his life would ever have managed to trip it. And that he'd just bounced off of, without causing an explosion.

A cable that was *much* too long and obvious to catch *people*.

Oh, no.

He heard the horse scream, off in the distance. A horse screaming was a terrible sound, one he never wanted to hear again.

Then he saw the dragon.

There hadn't been a dragon near the midlands in a hundred and fifty years. More to the point, there hadn't been an *angry* dragon—one with a couple of inconvenient holes blown into its hide from badly-aimed shrapnel—anywhere near *him* in, well, forever.

That's where the diamond came from, he thought idiotically. Old dragons had the things embedded in their hides from years of lying atop treasure hoards; the thing had probably just fallen out.

Run. Run run *run*.

The dragon was no longer distracted by the horse, and had nothing to focus on but Eleazar. Who fled, tripping over his own feet again and pulling himself up, trying to lose himself in the woods. The thing had already shown an ability to knock down trees but at least they would *slow it down*. He could hear it behind him, could hear the trees groan and crack as the huge beast's body slammed into them.

The treeline broke, and he saw the militia in the field. A solid front, musketeers and grenadiers at least; maybe some cavalry behind them somewhere. They would have been a relief if their guns hadn't been pointed his way. They wore green and blue; dragon-hunter's coats.

"FIRE!" came the command. He hit the ground, skidding as a hundred musket balls flew over his head and slammed into the dragon. This only made the thing angrier, but at least it distracted it from eating *him*. The dragon leapt over him, tearing great furrows in the earth with its claws as it headed for the infantry line.

He heard another command over the roars. "ARTILLERY!" Cannons chimed; another dozen booms, and the dragon took a face and chest full of close-range grapeshot. It hit the ground hard, skidding to a stop just in front of the infantry, who had dropped their muskets and switched to pikes. The pikemen rushed to finish the dragon, but the cannons had done their work; the giant creature was dead.

Eleazar got to his feet, stumbling toward the soldiers, who gave him a once-over and pointed him toward their captain.

"Congratulations," the captain said. He wore a fancy hat along with his uniform, which hadn't a spot of mud on it. Eleazar was filthy, wet and cold from having hit the ground so many times in the last half-hour. "You flushed the beast out of the woods; we thought we'd be taking all night getting it to come out after us."

"Accident," Eleazar said. "My horse stepped on part of the hoard; got it caught in a shoe. I think the thing was stalking us. I'm so glad you're here."

"You're entitled to part of the bounty, you know," the captain said. "Enough to keep you flush for a decade or more."

"I'll trade part of it for a new horse right now," Eleazar said. "And a medic's kit, if you have one." He still had a job to do. There was disease waiting for him, and now he had to buy Allan a new horse.

Ramtucko was still a couple of hours away. Who knew what he'd run into between now and then.

*   *   *

The Disconnected

This is the story of the day I didn't die.

I know. That's most days. Every day, actually, except for one, and when that day happens you don't actually get to be the one telling the story. Well, trust me. Roll with it.

My name is Elena Irizarri. I was about to be— half an hour away, maybe—the most famous nerd in human history. *My face next to 'nerd' in the dictionary* level famous. *Who is this 'Gates' person?* famous. All I had to do was walk out on stage as soon as my introduction was finished, wave, walk through one door, and walk out

Balremesh and other stories

another.

The doors were fifteen feet apart, and I wouldn't be walking through the space in between. That was the tricky part. We had finally cracked it: human teleportation, across, at least in theory, unlimited distance.

The guy doing my introduction was a billionaire. He was one of maybe half a dozen extraordinarily wealthy people who had poured truly unseemly amounts of cash into the enterprise my father and uncle had started decades ago, and of the original moneybags who were still alive he'd donated the most, so he got to bask in the attention as we proved ourselves to the world.

Sadly, neither Dad nor Uncle Epigmenio were around to witness the proceedings. Dad had passed away fifteen years ago, and Tío Epi ... well, that's a long story, one that ends with *he wasn't allowed on the premises any longer*. Dad had come up with the theoretical underpinnings of teleportation in grad school, and had followed it with a monomania that would have landed all of us in the poorhouse had he not made friends with the sole scion of one of the wealthiest families on the East Coast. The Humboldts knew genius when they saw it, and they also saw ancillary benefits when they saw them. They bankrolled Dad's experiments until those side benefits started producing money on their own, and after that investors never stopped calling.

Here's how teleportation works, in a nutshell: first, an

object is transformed into a data stream on a molecular level. Then that data stream is piped at the speed of light to what is effectively a giant 3D printer some distance away. That 3D printer rebuilds the object. Kapow! Instantaneous (well, *really fast*) travel across intense distances.

Every single word in that sentence was impossible when Dad got started. Moving the data *alone*—a small rock needed *terabytes* of data to properly replicate—required innovations in data storage and transfer that made Moore's Law slow and obsolete and basically rebuilt the entire communications industry from the ground up. Along the way, we invented *replication*, which was easier than teleportation—because you needed to be able to scan something on a molecular level and then rebuild a perfect copy *before* you even tackled the question of *moving* that data. *That* shook up entire industries too, although it was expensive and complicated enough that it hadn't come close to being widely available yet.

By the time Dad was 60 and I was 10—it took him a while to get around to having a family—they had managed to transform most of Puerto Rico into a tech hub and he was ready to start trials with living things. By the time I was old enough to help with the family business, we were starting to think about moving on to vertebrates. God, the fights we had with ethics boards, *every step of the way*, and the painstaking work needed to make sure that the animals weren't feeling pain, that they were maintaining their memories, that what came out of one teleporter was *really the same creature* as the one that went in—and all the work necessary to handle the step up in *object complexity* that came along with it. Even a simple worm is an order of magnitude more complicated than any artificial object. A goat? Forget about it.

Okay, I guess I got around to Tío Epi after all: he started secret animal trials *way* before we were ready, and hid them from all of us. He was in his nineties now; I hadn't seen him in decades but from all reports he was still hale and hearty and basically hated everyone connected with the company.

I snapped out of my reverie long enough to listen to Bill Humboldt's speech for a few minutes. He wasn't even a third of the way through; I'd seen the final draft. Still plenty of time to wait.

Interesting things happen when you start talking about teleporting people. We'd done everything we could, as I said to ensure that the animal at one end of a 'port was the same animal at the other end. We'd tested memory, personality, we'd given an animal a command and then teleported it and then watched as the animal that came out the other side performed that command, everything we could think of. And, amazingly, we'd done it without very many catastrophic failures, a fun euphemism that meant "dead animals." As it worked out, all the safety protocols we'd built into object teleportation meant that trying and failing to transport a living thing just meant that *nothing happened*—a partially successful teleport, which is *way* grosser than you think it is no matter how active your imagination is—was an incredibly rare occurrence.

But yeah. The problem was people. People have *souls*. Or maybe they don't! It's not like we'd managed to *find* the things, or empirically demonstrate their existence or their non-existence. But even if we don't *really* have souls, we certainly *think* and *feel like* we have souls, and it turns out that a whole lot of people have real problems with the idea that they could literally be broken down into zeroes and ones and rebuilt and the thing that was rebuilt was still *them*. More people were willing to simply *die* than have some other thing with their memories and personality running around *pretending* to be them, *convinced* it was them—and once that idea of teleportation took root in someone's head, it was damned hard to dislodge it.

So the "human trials" portion of the process just sort of … never happened. We couldn't *make* anyone be a subject, and no ethics board anywhere would approve the trials, and even an attempt to get some death row prisoners to volunteer got shot down by the government. We'd made Puerto Rico a *state* and they still wouldn't let us.

Which was why the first human teleported was going to be me. In front of an exclusive gathering of several hundred people. And on live TV.

I really, really hoped it was going to work.

The crowd went nuts. I'd spaced out again; apparently Bill was done with his speech, and there was a handler approaching me with a mildly worried *you probably need to get your butt on stage now* look on his face.

I wasn't supposed to talk. I had a speech in my pocket, but I wasn't to say a word until the performance was over.

There were two teleportation pods on the stage. The first was at stage level, but the second was on poles, several feet above the ground, with a little stairway off to the side. It had been pointed out to us that doing a teleportation trick on a stage would look exactly like every magician's trick ever employed for hundreds of years; we hoped that by lifting the destination pod a few feet up would sufficiently prove that I hadn't just climbed down through the stage.

I shook hands with Bill and waved to the crowd and then went to the first pod. They'd told me that what with trying to whip the crowd into a frenzy and basic showmanship I should expect about two minutes between going into the first pod and coming out of the second. It would *take* a little bit longer than that; the data transfer time was nearly nonexistent at this distance but I wouldn't perceive any of that.

I wouldn't be able to hear or see a thing once going inside the pod; animal trials had shown that it was best if the pods were complete sensory deprivation chambers.

Being in one place and then being in a completely different place in the blink of an eye had proved to be highly agitating to our more intelligent test subjects.

So I stood there in the dark. Two minutes was an *incredibly* long time when you couldn't see or hear anything, so I did a countdown in my head. At about the 2:30 mark I felt a painful ripple across my entire body. It hurt more than I had expected, actually; we'd sent animals through with sensors embedded in their brains and they generally didn't show much of a pain response at all, although there was clearly a sensory component to being ripped apart and being put back together.

Okay. I was across, and I'd survived. Now to wait for the door to open.

And about ten seconds later, it did. The sudden bright light meant it took a moment to orient myself and realize something had gone terribly wrong.

I was still in the first pod. I hadn't moved. The test was a failure.

So why was everyone applauding so loudly? Bill Humboldt had never looked happier. The crowd was on their feet and everyone was going *nuts*.

And Bill was pointing at the *second* pod. No one was looking at me.

No one.

What the hell was going on? I took a couple of steps out of my pod, surprised at how shaky my knees were. I hadn't even *written* a "well, that didn't work" speech.

And then watched as I stepped out of the *second* pod, reaching out to take Bill's hand as I walked down the stairs. The other me had shaky knees, too.

My hair looks terrible, I thought, ridiculously.

I didn't know what to do. No one could *see* me.

"Bill!" I shouted. No reaction. I started shouting to myself and abruptly realized I didn't know what to call *me*. I just walked over, standing right behind Bill, watching as I came down the stairs.

Bill turned, letting go of my hand, and walked *straight through me* on his way back to the podium.

And the other one—the other *me*—it looked at me. Straight in the eye.

And it *winked*.

And it walked through me on the way to the podium, pulled my speech out of my pocket, and delivered it. Flawlessly. I stood there in disbelief as it happened.

What had we done?

*　　*　　*

Warrior Jayashree and the Gallows Pole

A devilishly persistent beam of sunlight dragged the warrior Jayashree into unwilling consciousness. She tried to cover her eyes, to snatch a paltry few moments more sleep away from the accursed daytime, only to realize she couldn't move her arm.

Either of her arms.

It occurred to her that the bed she was lying in was exceedingly uncomfortable, and that her head did not appear to rest on a pillow.

I'm in gaol again, aren't I?

She forced an eye open. She winced painfully, as the action allowed a bit more of the demon sunrise into her skull.

I'm probably in gaol, and I may also still be a bit drunk.

Drunk was good. It meant she had probably at least earned the imprisonment somehow. Hopefully whatever had gotten her arrested had been fun.

She gathered the dregs of her strength and wrenched her other eye open, trying to look around her cell—for that was certainly what it was—while moving her eyes and her head as little as possible. She was dressed in a light, coarse shift that she was certain didn't belong to her. She was laying on a stone bench set into a wall, and her arms were secured by bamboo rope tied to a metal ring. The window the offending sunbeam was pestering her through was barred.

Gaol. Definitely gaol.

She tested the ropes. They would break, if she really needed them to, although she might have to accept spraining a wrist along the way. Her legs were unbound. She had enough slack to sit up, so she did. Started to, at least, until a thousand tiny homunculi wielding icepicks declared war upon on her temples and she sank back against the bench again.

Perhaps a few minutes more, before I try again.

She heard motion behind her, and the closing of a heavy door.

"So. What did I do?" she asked. Her voice sounded much more like a croak than she was used to.

"You don't *remember*?" The voice was familiar. And quite irritated. It sounded like—

Oh, no.

Ignoring her body's protests, she rolled off the bench and into the closest approximation her muscles and bound wrists would allow of a genuflect. It hurt more than she expected. And in more places.

This isn't just a hangover. Oh, it was certainly a hangover, and probably one caused by grape sura. Grape sura always hurt the worst the next day. But there was something else wrong. She'd been in a fight.

"Who did I kill?"

"Stand up," the voice answered, and the ropes slithered away from her wrists like snakes. She turned toward the voice and dropped closer to the ground.

"Mother of Magic. My deepest apologies for whatever has—"

"Stand. UP."

She leapt to her feet, the voice compelling her, her limbs and torso screaming in protest.

The Mother of Magic stood before her, practically glowing in head-to-toe white raiment.

White. White was the color of mourning. The Mother of Magic generally wore ruby-red.

Ohhhh, this is bad.

"Look out the window." This statement did not carry

the compulsion along with it, but Jayashree did not hesitate.

Her cell overlooked a central courtyard, which was not unexpected. The gallows pole standing in the center of the courtyard was, though.

Jayashree cleared her throat, concentrating intensely on willing her hangover away.

"Is … is that for me?"

"At the moment? Yes. And I am not sure I should do anything to help you *change* that, either." Jayashree turned, daring to look the Mother of Magic in the eyes. Her pupils were gone, her eyes a shining white void against ebony skin.

This was generally not a good sign.

"May I ask what happened?"

"Do you recall being propositioned last night?"

"I am propositioned every night," Jayashree said. "I don't … wait…"

She recalled a particular man, not unlovely to look at, but with food in his beard and the stink of fish on his breath. A man who had loomed over her, trying to intimidate her with his size. She had … what had she done? She genuinely didn't remember.

"Possibly one. Large. Unkempt."

"You have bedded the unkempt before, Jayashree. More than once, I believe."

"I didn't want to bed this one," she said, shrugging. "He felt differently. I take it I overreacted?"

"Somewhat. He went through a table on his way to the floor. A piece of the table lodged itself behind his ear. I suspect you did not intend to kill him."

Jayashree thought about this. It sounded familiar.

"And then ... and then, he had a *lot* of friends, for some reason..." Yes, there had definitely been a fight. She'd clearly held her own; nothing was broken. She tested her teeth with her tongue. Some missing, but none newly so.

"The nephew of the Rajh."

Ah.

"That's bad."

"It is. The Rajh is rather put out about it."

I can imagine. "And you?"

The Mother of Magic shrugged, her first human gesture since entering the room. "I have met the nephew. He was a boor. I can see why you rejected his advances."

She forced more of the alcohol's aftereffects out of her brain. "Is there to be a trial? Or are we discussing escape and not defense?"

"The Rajh has a proposition for you," the Mother of Magic said. "I suspect he believes it to be a death sentence of a sort. But he has a proposition."

"I accept," Jayashree said.

"Yes, you do," the Mother of Magic said. "And then, when you are released, *I* will kill you. This has been a most inconvenient morning, Jayashree."

Jayashree bowed her head.

"Mistress," she said.

*   *   *

"Were this not your creature, Mother Manisha, I would have dealt with her already," the Rajh said. "You should keep better track of your guards. *Her* survival is due solely to my high opinion of *you*." He fingered his seal of office, which dangled heavily around his neck.

"Your high opinion of my office, at least," the Mother of Magic replied calmly. There was no love lost between her and the Rajh. They were both fully aware of this fact but of the two he was more likely to pretend to conceal it. "The Potentate will frown upon open warfare between his Rajh and his *goddess'* Mother of Magic."

Jayashree knelt facedown, in a warrior's tunic and loose pantaloons, trying to stay as close to the ground as possible. The Mother of Magic had released her from her cell and given her less than an hour to make herself dressed and presentable. She had forced herself to have some greasy food and cold coffee to wash away the last dregs of the hangover, and now her stomach complained. Not so loudly, she hoped, that the other two could hear it. Her arms and armor had not been restored to her yet, but if the Rajh genuinely expected a task from her she would surely get them back soon.

"You suggested you had a task for my *creature* to perform," the Mother reminded the Rajh. "One that might, somehow, soothe the pain of the loss of your nephew, which you surely feel so keenly." "I am shattered," the Rajh said, and Jayashree realized with a jolt that this had nothing to do with her or even with his nephew. The Rajh was simply looking for someone expendable and she had obligingly provided herself for him. Her loss being an inconvenience to the Mother would simply be a bonus in the man's eyes.

The Mother did not rise to the bait. "The task, then?"

"Rise, warrior," he said, and Jayashree climbed to her feet, trying to keep from groaning or wincing too obviously. There were scrapes and bruises mottling the red-wheat color of her skin on her face and arms. She would not let him think they mattered.

"Are you familiar with the pishacha?" he asked.

Jayashree barely suppressed a sideways glance at the Mother. The question was unexpected. "Demon spirits," she said. "They haunt graves and cremation grounds. They ... I do not recall, Rajh, whether they are the type to possess the living, or merely to consume them. I am sorry." She bowed her head.

"Both," the Rajh said. "There is a cremation ground not far outside the walls. It has of late become infested with them. They are beginning to spill outside the grounds and bother travelers and others. People are beginning to talk. You are to rid me of these ... upsetting presences. Do this task, I care not how, and I will forget your offense upon my family."

"Upon one of the lesser branches, to be sure," the Mother of Magic added. Rather unhelpfully, Jayashree felt.

The Rajh ignored the jab.

"How does one defeat a pishacha?" Jayashree asked. "I have never encountered such a thing."

"Cold iron will do, I am told," the Rajh answered. "But silver would be better. A pity, then, that I have no silvered weapons to spare to you."

"The Mother will provide," the Mother of Magic said. "We will outfit Jayashree properly ourselves, and send a contingent of warriors today."

"She is to perform the task alone," the Rajh said placidly.

"And why?" the Mother challenged. "It seems that your *problem* would be solved more easily were we to send more than a single greenwood warrior."

"The pishacha are shy," the Rajh said. "They have not appeared to *groups*, only to individual travelers. A larger group would likely go unbothered."

"Then someone more seasoned," the Mother protested. "A more experienced warrior. One who could, again, *solve your problem.*"

"The pishacha or the gallows pole," the Rajh countered. "Those are your choices. Those, and no others."

Jayashree bowed her head, and made her choice.

*　　*　　*

"The blade is silvered," the Mother said, "and the dagger cold iron. You will not need your bow. You will be too close to them to use it, when they finally reveal themselves."

"Any suggestions on tactics?" Jayashree asked. She tightened the straps on her armor, not sure if she was wasting her time or not. She had been in fights, even a few battles, but none against the undead.

The Mother murmured a few words, pressing a thumb into Jayashree's forehead. Jayashree closed her eyes as the world opened to her for a moment, then snapped closed again. "The pishacha have their own language," she said. "And you will *feel* them talking before you hear it. The word *pishacha* is an old one; it means *chatterers*. The spell will help you understand their words, if they wish to be understood at all. Listening to them may save you from battle. If it comes to iron and silver, be merciless. Every blow must be a killing one. Aim for the neck. They are not human, but they will die like humans if they must. And trust *all* of your senses. If you feel one nearby, swing, whether you see it or not."

"It sounds like you are telling me *not* to trust my eyes," Jayashree said.

The Mother considered. "Not quite. They can make themselves invisible to your eyes. They *cannot* create illusions of themselves. If you see one, it is there. If you do not see one, it may *still* be there."

"I am not ready," Jayashree admitted.

"None of us ever are," the Mother replied. "But I have faith in you, daughter. We will meet again, I promise you."

Jayashree nodded, and strapped the silvered khanda to her hip.

*   *   *

The old cremation grounds were a few miles outside of town, at a sharp bend in the river. For generations, bodies had been ritually burnt on the muddy spit of land the river encircled, and any cremains not borne away by the wind were commended to the water a few days later. The Grove of the Children was across the river; the bodies of the young were buried, not burned. Jayashree found herself hoping the pishacha were on the cremation side, as killing the reanimated spirits of children felt like a task heavy enough to break her.

She considered riding and decided to walk. She suspected the pishacha would not emerge until nighttime, which meant she had several hours. The day had grown hot but dreary, a thick layer of clouds rolling in over the bright sun that had awakened her in the morning. It would rain soon enough. *I may as well die in the rain*, Jayashree thought, and considered simply continuing past the cremation grounds and never returning. The Rajh would likely assume she had died. The Mother of Magic would know, of course. The Mother of Magic had a way of always eventually knowing *everything*. Jayashree was not sure she would go to the trouble to track her down again.

No. She had killed before, but always intentionally. The Rajh's nephew was the first whose death she had caused by accident. She felt shame as she realized she had not bothered to find out the man's name. He had likely introduced himself, but the drink had erased the memory. The Rajh had not bothered to use his name, either. If this was the task she must perform to atone for the death she had caused, she would try her best to do it, even if it felt a bit unreasonable.

She ate a light meal a few hundred yards from the cremation grounds, enough to keep her strength until well after dark. She had seen no one since leaving the city, and it looked as if no one had passed by here in some time. The path was overgrown, no tracks of horse or man or cart beating down the underbrush.

Odd. The Rajh had said the spirits were bothering passersby. There was no sign there had been any for weeks, at least. Not for the first time, Jayashree wished she had spent more of her time learning woodcraft.

She looked up at the sky. The rain would come soon, before nightfall.

I will not die today, she thought. That day would

come eventually, but she would not die wet and cold. At least being at the cremation grounds meant there was plenty of wood available to build a fire. She set out to prepare for her vigil. The fire would have to be large, to keep the rain from extinguishing it.

*　　*　　*

She felt a cold touch, a brush across the back of her neck. She had been meditating by the fire for hours, cross-legged, the expected rain never growing stronger than an annoying sprinkle. She opened her eyes and rose to her feet in one motion, one hand on her khanda.

She saw nothing, but she heard whispers all around her. They were *almost* understandable, as if the pishacha were deliberately concealing their words from her.

"Show yourselves," she said. Her words vanished into the silence, as the spirits around her stopped speaking.

Then they started again, and this time she could understand them.

you
what what are you
what is this
it has a sword it has a sword a weapon a weapon to kill
kill it bring it down into the ground
it hears us
do you do you hear us do you hear our words

we must kill it

no not yet

no

soon

do you hear us

"I hear you, honored spirits," Jayashree said, cold fear working its way up her spine.

you were sent to kill

no not to kill

to kill

to listen

it fears

it was sent to listen it hears and understands

it was sent to kill it carries a sword the sword bites and shines and bites and shines and bites and shines and bites

to kill to kill to kill

fear

fear

it fears

Jayashree unsheathed her sword, plunging it into the embers of her fire. There was a sudden storm of noise around her, then a withdrawal. She waited, making no further movements, and felt the spirits growing closer to her again.

"I was sent to kill," she said. "But I have free will. I will listen if you will speak. I was told you had become a danger to the living. That you should be removed from this place. That you have killed travelers, and menaced the living."

She felt more cold touches, but nothing caused her to reach for the sword again. A shape coalesced in front of her, a swirl of smoke slowly forming into a familiar shape. The babble of voices began again.

lies

your words are lies

it will kill us take it take it now

it will not

it speaks lies

but it wishes for truth

kill it kill it kill it kill it

no

not yet

Jayashree felt a pressure at the back of her neck, a beckoning, an invitation. *Trust all of your senses*, the Mother of Magic had told her.

"Tell me what you want," she said.

quiet

silence

we wish quiet quiet the grave the silence the sound of peace

but not by the sword no not the sword not hurting not biting not silver

can you bring us this

can you can you can you

will you

kill it kill it kill it kill it kill it now
will you bring us
the quiet

"Tell me how," she said, and felt the pressure at the back of her neck again.

She had asked the Rajh if the pishacha were creatures who possessed or merely killed. *Both*, he had answered. The shape formed in the smoke again, and the rain fell harder.

This is not the day I die, she thought to herself again, and let the pishacha have her.

*　　*　　*

The visions came upon her all at once in a wave. She panicked and tried to push them away, and they abated for just a moment. The pishacha appeared to understand that she could not cope with them all at once. But then the memories began to arrive one at a time, no pauses in between, and every memory ending in death and blood, and that was almost worse, for when those who had become the pishacha died, Jayashree died with them. If she had caused one death by accident, she had atoned for it fully within minutes, as she died over and over again in their visions.

And each time, the same face. Sometimes wielding a dagger, or a spear, or a garrote. Sometimes standing nearby and smiling as an innocent swung from a rope.

Sometimes giving orders that, followed obediently, led to painful death at the talons of his other victims. The same face. The same hands, bloody from murder upon murder. The same result, as the spirits of the unjust dead rose again, waiting for the one who could understand them, the one who could end their pain, who could avenge them.

him
always him
he was the one
all of us hurt
all blood
all murder all blood all death
trapped here in the cold and the wet and the cold and the wet
do you understand
do you do you do you do you see
do you see
"I see," Jayashree said.
will you help
"I will," she answered.
Everything went black.

*   *   *

She felt herself flying, moving faster than she could imagine, and hurtled into a building, through halls and up stairs. She finally came back to herself back in the city, standing in a room, at the foot of a bed. The storm roared outside. The bed was opulent, surrounded by a gossamer curtain. The room furnished as if for a man of wealth.

And she knew where she was, somehow. *The Rajh's bedroom.* She shuddered. How had they brought her here? And so quickly?

They cannot see us, the pishacha told her, speaking as one voice for the first time. *The pishacha are hidden to groups,* she thought. And she had been, for a time, one of them. She dropped a hand to her hip, feeling the khanda hanging back at her side again. Its pommel was still warm, the metal still retaining some of the heat of the fire, unaffected by the cold and wet of the storm.

"He had guards," she whispered. "Did we kill them?"

They sleep. They cannot see us, and they sleep. He is yours.

She unsheathed her khanda, and swept the curtain aside. The Rajh slept peacefully, wrapped in expensive silk pajamas.

The pajamas tore as she grabbed him by his tunic and lifted him above her head one-handed, undead energies bolstering her strength.

His first reaction was to call, panicked, for his guards. She let him, staring into his eyes. No one would hear him. Let him call.

"You lied to me," she said.

"I did nothing," he said. "I sent you to kill spirits. You let them *have* you. I can see it in your *eyes.*" He struggled against her grip.

"And the Mother of Magic let me *understand* them," Jayashree answered. "They showed me how they died. They showed me who *killed* them. Your symbol of office. All of their deaths. *You*, responsible. And you'd have added me to their ranks without a second thought. You've been executing any who cross you for *years,* making them disappear at the old cremation grounds. None of them with a trial. And few for any real offense."

"As is my *right*," the Rajh replied, choking. "I rule here. *I.* Not the spirits, and not the Mother of Magic's *lapdogs.*"

"They seem to disagree," Jayashree answered, and there was a crack of lightning, and suddenly she stood outside, the rain now falling so hard it hurt. The gallows pole still stood at the center of the courtyard, seven steps leading up to the platform. She held the Rajh two feet off the ground as if he was a kitten, her muscles feeling no strain. The voices of the pishacha were legion again, echoing in her head.

do it

yes yes yes

hurt him burn him kill him

he was the one

we died he dies

give him to us

give him to the ground

do it do it do it

Realizing where he was, the Rajh began to scream.

"You said to rid you of the spirits," Jayashree spat. "You cared not how, do you remember? The spirits will trouble you no longer, Rajh. There is just this one thing to do, first."

Jayashree hauled the struggling man up the seven steps. At the top, the rope beckoned.

"The pishacha or the gallows pole, you told me," the warrior Jayashree said, wrapping the bamboo rope around the Rajh's neck. "I made the wrong choice at first. I have changed my mind. I choose the *pole*."

She kicked the Rajh in the back, sending him flying off the platform.

The wet snap of his neck echoed like thunder in the empty courtyard.

* * *

Luther M. Siler

Warrior Jayashree and the Young

The room reeked of rice beer and coconut wine, the odor wafting out even before he brushed open the thick woolen curtain that marked the bedroom's threshold. The servant listened carefully, letting his eyes adjust to the darkness inside before speaking. The room was sparsely furnished, containing a large bed, a chair, and a couple of small tables, one of which had been knocked over. Clothing was scattered everywhere, along with other items that perhaps ought not to be stored on the floor or haphazardly tossed into corners.

Hm. *Too much* clothing. He squinted, looking more carefully at the bed. Someone shifted, a beam of light from the courtyard getting past the curtain and landing on a patch of wheat-colored skin.

He raised an eyebrow. *The mistress is not alone.* Well, it couldn't be helped. He cleared his throat.

There was a groan, and more shifting from within the room.

"You are needed, mistress. It is important."

Someone threw a pillow, which glanced off the curtain. Another groan. He pulled the curtain aside entirely, flooding the room with light. There was a squeal, and the mistress' guest tumbled off the bed onto the floor, pulling a sheet over herself.

"I should take your manhood for that, Mitesh," the mistress growled. Her voice was deeper than usual, almost sounding congested.

"As you wish, mistress," Mitesh responded evenly. This threat was issued at last a few times a week and as of yet she had not followed through.

The mistress rolled out of bed, one hand held firmly against the side of her head. She glared at Mitesh, making no move to cover herself.

"And who has arrived to *need* me at this hour of the day?"

"It is past noon, mistress."

"There are knives in here somewhere, Mitesh. Do not make me find them."

"You are about to step on one, mistress." Her urumi was at her feet, unwound. It was not a weapon one would be pleased to place bare feet upon. The mistress cast her eyes downward and collected the urumi, winding the flexible blades around her waist and clipping the handle to them. It was a most dangerous belt, with no cloth underneath to protect her from the edges.

"No more remarks, Mitesh. Tell me who is here and why."

"She said to give you this, mistress," he said, holding out a small wooden box. He took a few steps into the room and nearly tripped over yet another prone figure, this one a man. He had burrowed into a pile of clothing during the night. The man did not react to being kicked.

Mitesh looked more closely. "Is this one dead?"

"I don't think so," she said. "Although I expect he'll wish he was when he wakes up. Can t hold his liquor." The mistress took the box, her mouth curled in scorn, and opened it. Mitesh watched as much of the influence of the rice beer drained from her face, replaced with deep alarm and concern. And, unbelievably, something that looked very much like fear.

She closed the box again, handing it back to Mitesh, and glanced over at her other bedmate, who was still curled on the floor by the bed. Mitesh thought it entirely possible that the girl had fallen back to sleep.

"Wh--" She stopped, clearing her throat.

"Who *precisely* is our guest, Mitesh?"

"The scholar Ansuya, mistress."

The mistress nodded.

"Feed ... ah ... feed them both, and get her home somehow," she said. "Let him worry about himself." She shook her head, wincing, trying to clear the cobwebs of the night's revelry from her head and not quite succeeding. "Tell our guest I will meet with her presently." She turned away from Mitesh, he and her night's partners all but forgotten, searching for the rest of her clothing among the riot of discarded laundry on the floor.

Then she paused, and stood up, a quizzical look on her face. "There may be a third. Somewhere. See if either of them remembers. You'll know what to do, right? You always do."

Mitesh nodded, and when his mistress went back to searching for her clothes he looked inside the box. It contained the hand of a small child, roughly torn off at the wrist, set carefully atop a bed of bloodstained white cotton. The nails on four of the fingers were cut evenly and carefully painted. The fifth finger was missing.

*   *   *

"Ansuya."

The scholar stood, nodding at her host, who bowed deeply. They had met in a sitting room adjoining the courtyard on the house's second floor. The room had several windows, and a pleasant breeze did its best to dispel the afternoon heat and humidity.

"Warrior Jayashree. I trust you have recovered from your ... sudden illness?"

Jayashree winced. Mitesh had been instructed many times to keep visitors away from her, and preferably out of the house altogether, when she was in her cups. That instruction had not been meant to apply to the scholar for any number of reasons, but the man had done his best anyway.

"I am well enough, scholar. What has happened?"

"The hand was carried into the village by a dog. Several girls are missing. That is all we have found of any of them."

Jayashree raised an eyebrow. "A matter for the authorities, not for a scholar. You are leaving something out."

"Did you remove the hand from the box?"

"I did not." She looked around, suddenly wondering what she'd done with it. Wordlessly, Mitesh appeared next to her and silently gave her the box. She opened it again, with far more care this time, and looked at the hand again.

"Look at the palm," Ansuya said.

Jayashree carefully took the hand from the box and turned it over. There was a symbol carefully carved into the palm. Parts of the hand had been flayed to add detail to the image.

"What is that?" she said. The symbol *itself* made her uneasy, somehow, even without considering its macabre source.

"Rotate the hand. Point the fingers toward you."

She turned the hand, and the nature of the shape became clear.

The skull of a goat.

Jayashree's eyes widened and her nostrils flared.

"Tell me what this is," she said.

"The work of a cult," the scholar said. "This was no animal. Do you understand, now, why they came to me, and why I came to you?"

"Let Mitesh know where the dog was found," Jayashree said. "I will be there within the hour."

There were preparations to be made.

*   *   *

The day's heat was already brutal, yet Jayashree felt a chill despite her armor. Mitesh had directed her to the central square of a nearby village, and Ansuya stood there to greet her, surrounded by a small mob of stone-faced villagers. Jayashree surveyed them. The crowd appeared to be made up almost entirely of children and the elderly. Not a man or woman among them had the look of a laborer, much less a warrior.

They are elsewhere, then. Ansuya will have news. She began to dismount her horse, a motion Ansuya halted with a quick gesture. Jayashree directed a raised eyebrow toward the scholar.

"News both good and bad." Ansuya said. "The good news is that they have located where the girls were taken already. The bad? We have lost another. Come. We must hurry." The old woman gestured, and a young boy brought her a second horse. She mounted fluidly, an impressively graceful movement from someone of her age, and kicked the horse in the flanks. Jayashree twitched the reins and squeezed her knees together, and her horse followed.

"How well do you know this country?" Ansuya asked as Jayashree's horse pulled alongside her.

"Well enough," Jayashree said. Or, at least, she'd have known it well enough if she were fully sober yet. The horse had done most of the navigating. Mitesh had made her his elixir again but it hadn't fully kicked in yet.

"There is a ravine not far from here," Ansuya said. "The girl who was taken today has a younger brother. He followed the kidnappers. He says they disappeared into a stone wall."

"That seems ... unlikely," Jayashree replied. "But the boy was likely terrified. Perhaps he misunderstood what he was seeing."

"Perhaps," Ansuya answered.

"What was that symbol, scholar? Who would do that to a little girl?"

"I have heard of this before," Ansuya said. "But not in

a long while, and only from scattered references in song, or from the oldest of my codices. They are called the *Young,* and their gods are ancient and cruel. Long has human sacrifice been among their rituals."

"That hand was from no clean sacrifice," Jayashree responded. "That child was torn apart."

"We do not yet know what their sacrifice was <u>to</u>," Ansuya said, "Or what happened afterward."

Jayashree did not respond, goading her horse into greater speed instead.

*   *   *

A small crowd of people surrounded an outcropping in the ravine wall. For the second time, Jayashree appraised the crowd. This was clearly nearly all of the able-bodied in the village. Farmers and workers, all of them, strong of arm and back but armed with little more than spears and scythes, with naught a protective garment or steel blade among them. A man detached himself from the crowd and spoke with Ansuya, his voice too low for Jayashree to hear. The group regarded her with a mixture of fear and hope, a few tightening their grips on their weapons as she approached. This was not a crowd accustomed to battle, but they would fight for her if she allowed them.

Ansuya nodded, patting the man on his back with one hand and turning to Jayashree.

"Come, look at this," she said. Jayashree dismounted

and followed the scholar, who was walking around to the blind side of the outcropping.

The stone protrusion concealed a cave entrance. A cold breeze blew from the entrance, carrying with it an unsettling scent of rot and blood.

"They went in through here," she said.

"And has no one followed them?' Jayashree replied, shocked at their cowardice. "How many could possibly be hidden inside? The child could have been killed while they waited!"

"They sent five," Ansuya said. "Their strongest, and the most eager to fight. None have returned. Some claim that they heard screams."

Jayashree listened carefully. She heard nothing. Not so much as the sound of a bird, or the skittering of a rodent from inside the cave. The pounding of her own blood in her temples was the loudest thing anywhere near her.

"Find me torches, and someone to carry them," she said. "My hands will be full." She returned to her horse.

She had brought more equipment than she needed, unsure of the challenges that she would be facing. Her bamboo longbow was left with the horse, unstrung. A bow would be nearly useless inside of a cave. She kept her khanda and a dagger with her. The khanda was a two-edged blade, a shade over three feet in length, that widened from the hilt out to a blunted point at the other end. A wicked spike beneath the hilt served as a short-range weapon or a secondary grip to use the sword two-handed. She strapped a buckler shield to her left forearm, leaving her hand free, and placed her helmet upon her head.

She laid a hand on the grip of her urumi, still coiled around her waist, considering. The urumi was a weapon that demanded a lot of room to be used effectively, and with others fighting alongside her it could be just as dangerous to her friends as to her enemies. But it was a mark of her achievement as a warrior. The weapon was considered so dangerous to the wielder that only the most accomplished of fighters dared to learn its use. She still had several scars from inattentive moments during her training.

She left the weapon at her waist, adjusting it for easier access, and smoothed out the plates of her armor, which were sandwiched between layers of silk. Its weight was oppressive in the heat, but the cool of the cave would soon leave her comfortable enough.

"Enough," she murmured to herself. She was prepared or she was not. Further delay was pointless.

Four men and two women waited at the entrance of the cave. Three of them bore torches. The others carried their weapons only. Half of them were armed with nothing more dangerous than simple clubs. The others bore spears and a hand scythe.

"If there is negotiation to be done, I do it," she said. "If there is to be bloodshed, I strike the first blow. These are the only rules. If you do not plan to follow them, let me know now." She made eye contact with each of the six, who returned her gaze, if perhaps a bit nervously. Seven of them, then. A good number. Surely their numbers could not be overmatched inside the cave.

Jayashree turned without another word, striding into the cave and assuming her soldiers would follow her.

*   *   *

It took only a moment for her eyes to adjust to the torchlit darkness of the cave. The entrance was perfectly mundane, as the narrow entryway broadened to perhaps ten feet in width, with enough head room for the tallest man among them to walk comfortably. A quick examination of the space revealed some signs of use: a few discarded animal nests and some signs that people had camped there from time to time as well.

"There's no way out," one of the men with her said.

"Patience," Jayashree replied, an edge in her voice. "They were seen entering. They were not seen exiting. You did not even know this cave was *here*. Surely another exit could elude us for a moment."

"Here," called one of the torchbearers, a woman. She pointed to a wide beam of wood, incongruously embedded in a flat part of the wall. Her torch flickered madly; the odor was stronger here, and a wind blew from somewhere.

"A lintel," Jayashree murmured. "Good. There must be

a way to open it." She ran her hands over the lintel and the wall below it, seeking some sort of catch or release and finding nothing.

She pushed, experimentally, and felt the wall give.

"Here," she said, waving the others over. Three of them threw their weight against the wall, and the heavy stone gave way, swinging on a hidden pivot and allowing enough room to enter further into the cave. Behind it was a tunnel, barely wide enough for two to walk next to each other, the walls and ceiling heavily reinforced with more wooden beams. The work looked hurried, and dust drifted down from over their heads, disturbed by the motion of the door.

She heard a sound from ahead of them.

"Torchbearers to the back," she whispered. She pointed at the two who carried spears. "The two of you, behind me. Give me ten feet in front of you. And be *silent*." The spearholders nodded, their fear and resolve both clear on their faces.

She unsheathed her khanda and tightened her shield to her forearm, then crept ahead, grateful that she had left her noisy mail armor at home. The torches behind her provided just enough light to maneuver by, and soon enough the sounds ahead her resolved into voices.

Far too many voices.

She held out a hand, palm back, gesturing for those behind her to halt, and belly-crawled forward, peering around a corner into a room that seemed transported underground from a stone building. The floor was *tiled*, broad marbled pavers that filled the circular floor wall-to-wall. The walls were covered with draperies and, of all things, *mirrors*, the illumination in the room being provided by a single brazier. Standing next to the brazier was a single figure, cloaked in a black garment voluminous enough to make determining even its gender impossible, a shining golden medallion around its neck. Perhaps a dozen more cloaked individuals knelt on the floor in front of the high priest.

Against the wall to his left lay the shattered bodies of the five people that had been sent in before them.

The girl. Where was the *girl*?

Nowhere to be seen. Perhaps on the floor in front of the priest, but she couldn't see past the ones that were kneeling. The figures continued praying. She was close enough to pick out the words, but much of what they were saying made little sense to her.

"So from the wells of night to the gulfs of space, and from the gulfs of space to the wells of night, ever the praises of Great Cthulhu, of Tsathoggua, and of Him Who is not to be Named. Ever Their praises, and abundance to the Black Goat of the Jungles. Iä! Shub-Niggurath! The Goat with a Thousand Young!"

A wave of feeling washed over her, as the last trace of the coconut wine lost its hold, replaced by a nameless dread so deep it turned her bones to ice. For the briefest moment the veil of the world tore away, and what was exposed behind it was naught but madness and terror. Her panic was primal, beyond thought and reason and care and hope. Only one thing could protect her, only one thing could save her from the palpable madness beyond the veil.

"Iä..." she murmured to herself, beginning to let go. With the greatest of effort, she shook her head, pushing the veil away, trying to return to herself.

Two behind her were not so lucky.

"Iä! Iä! The Goat! The Black Goat of the Jungle, Radiant She of the Thousand Young! Iä! Iä! *Shub-Niggurath*, the Black Goat of the Jungle with a Thousand Young!"

She rolled out of the way just as the spear struck the ground where she lay. Had she still been there, it would have split her spine. Behind her, she could hear combat. Ahead of her, the cultists had become aware of their presence. The man who had tried to kill her stood over her, froth and blood dripping from his lips, unfathomable madness in his eyes, veins bulging in his face and arms. She kicked his legs out from under him and rolled toward him, smashing the edge of her buckler into his larynx as he hit the ground. He choked and died. She leapt to her feet, her khanda in her hand. The others looked at her, the other villager lost to madness dead at their feet.

"That was the signal," she said. "Defend yourselves." She spun, meeting the brunt of the cultists' charge. She split one from crotch to chin with her khanda, then slammed a second out of her way with her shield. She thought of her urumi, still belted to her waist. The weapon was superb for crowd control. Too bad she hadn't the room to use it.

She was fortunate in one way: the cultists were only armed with daggers, and not very long ones at that. She had the advantage. She felt the spearbearers coming behind her and forced her way into the ritual chamber, nearly skidding in a pool of blood on the way in. She deflected a wild swing with her shield, then took the cultist's head from his shoulders with a backswing. Another jumped on her back, his dagger already lost, and she threw herself backwards and bashed him into the wall, slamming her khanda's spike into his ribcage when he lost his grip. She glanced at the spearbearers. They were holding their own, and the club-and-scythe contingent was beating a cultist on the ground. Two of her people were injured, but not badly.

She looked around for the girl. There was a hole in the floor in front of the high priest, who had not joined the melee. The priest dipped a torch into the brazier and lowered it into the hole. Jayashree could see him chanting as he did so, the words coming from him sounding like no human speech she had ever encountered. The chanting grew louder, drowning out even the sounds of the fight.

Oh, no. No.

Cold blue flame erupted from the pit, and Jayashree could no longer tell whose screams she heard: those of the dying men and women around her, her own, or those of the child who, she now hoped, had been dead long before the rescuers ever made it into the room. Jayashree prayed that she had died of *anything* other than that obscene otherwordly fire.

A sphere appeared in the air above the fire. Darkness poured from the sphere as light from a lantern, and the mirrored walls now no longer kept the room as brightly lit as it had been. The brazier still burned, but not as strongly, and her warriors had dropped most of their torches. A cold wind blew, and Jayashree realized that the bad air, still stinking of rot and blood and burning flesh and hair, was being swept from the chamber by something far fouler.

The cultists reacted as one, disengaging from the fight and turning their faces to the hole in the air, their eyes wild, fixed on nothing, chanting in the same inhuman black speech as the priest. She had three fighters left, two men and a woman. They cut down the remaining cultists as they howled their prayers.

Jayashree leapt for the priest, her khanda flashing. The priest met her with his own dagger, and sparks burst from their weapons as they met. She kicked him in the chest, tossing him across the room, and lifted her blade above her head, screaming a wordless battle cry. The priest laughed, a repellent gurgling sound more animal than human, and crawled to his feet, barely evading another wild blow from Jayashree's weapon. He reversed his grip on his dagger and stabbed at her again. She blocked the blow with her shield, then pinned his arm against her side. The next swing from her sword took the arm off at the shoulder, a gout of black blood spraying from the wound. The third attack split his ribcage, embedding the shattered pieces of his medallion into his heart. The priest collapsed to the ground, dead.

His hood fell back from his face as he died. The sight caused Jayashree to step back in shock. Two goat's horns protruded from the forehead of a face that had forgotten how to be human some time ago, a putrid combination of features from man and goat that called to mind something born dead and quietly buried in the night.

"The Young," Jayashree whispered to herself. "They're not even *people*."

A keening sound filled the room, and the blue fire died down. She turned. The sphere was still there, the death of the mad priest of the Young having no effect on it. It shimmered, and she realized that she could see something inside it.

"It's a portal," she said.

"What do we do?" one of the surviving men asked.

She looked closer, fear gripping her entrails with an icy hand. The sphere looked out into a great city, far in the distance, but a city such as none on Earth had ever seen. Buildings of impossible geometry scraped the clouds, and a black sun somehow shone in the sky. Beyond the city, mountains, their summits knife-sharp.

Before the city, a field, as broad and plain and flat as could be imagined, and in that field was an army. An army of the Young, their misshapen faces uncloaked, their weapons long and sharp and steaming with unholy poisons.

The army roared, a sound that shook the rock around them, and advanced toward the portal.

"Go," Jayashree told the men, a strange calm falling over her. "Use your clubs. Take them from the dead if you need to. Bring down the tunnel behind us. I want a million tons of rock between the world and ... *that*."

"We won't have time," one of them said.

"I will gain you your time," she said, and hurled herself into the portal.

A cold knife lacerated her skin, the world flashed away, and yet she somehow landed on her feet.

She looked around. The portal hung in the air behind her, larger on this side than on hers, and she watched as the warriors on the other side scavenged clubs and fled for the safety of the tunnel. She turned to face the army, and for the first time saw what was at their center: a two-hundred-foot monstrosity of tentacle and horn and scale and tooth and claw, many-mouthed, gibbering incoherently and roaring at the sky. She felt its gravidity, and knew that the horrors around her were its true offspring.

Somewhere, a flute was playing.

Jayashree smiled. She would die today, and soon.

But there was *finally* room to use her urumi.

* * *

Balremesh

My name is Montgomery Vale, and I do not believe in magic.

I repeat myself: *I do not believe in magic.*

I do not believe in magic, and therefore nothing I am about to write can be true. I am an old man, asleep in my bed, and the night's ill humours are clearly affecting my dreams. I write to calm my nerves, to simply record the events of recent hours. For if I am sane—if any of this has truly happened—I must leave warning for others.

I write because I may be insane, for surely none of this can have happened.

I write because *the door must not be opened*.

It seems ages ago that I found the book, but it can scarcely have been more than a day. I found it in my own library, on the floor by the fireplace. It was a massive tome, five inches thick, bound in a curious, tooled leather. The cover bore a nameplate of a cracked material I could not identify bearing a single word: *Balremesh*.

I hesitated to open the book at first. Something about it seemed to warn me away. An unusual thought possessed me: I felt as if the thing hated me. At the time, I dismissed it, believing myself foolish. I set the book—heavier than it should have been—on my writing-desk and examined it. It was warm to the touch, no doubt from its proximity to the fire. It was, as I have said, bound in a dry, old, dark-stained leather that flaked away under pressure, engraved deeply with arcane signs and symbols such like I had never seen. Horrid carvings of alien, mutated insects and other crawling things, rendered in extraordinary detail, adorned the spine and the edges. The pages, hundreds of them, thick and discolored, were gilded with a reddish material. It was *incredibly* old.

Did the fire dim as I opened the book? I thought that it did. The fire went down and the darkness in the room increased, became a palpable thing, eager to peruse the book alongside me. And that sound! A sigh, perhaps, or a muted moan, no doubt from a servant in another room, or a mere figment of my imagination. Even then, as I first opened it, the laws of reality seemed changed. A book does not sigh, and its opening does not suppress the light of the fire. It does not because it *can* not.

I did not, at first, recognize the language the book was scribed in. I say "scribed" because surely no printer's press could have produced these lines of script; irregular, slanted, sometimes running across one another, all in a thin ink more red than black. The script seemed varied; sometimes cramped and blocky and in other places more fluid and open, in a number of different hands, obviously the work of madmen or deviants.

At first.

And then... and then, the text *changed*. It swam under my eyes, turned, and emerged as readable, if untrained, English. I recall blinking, rubbing my eyes. I recall the impression that I had simply not been looking at the words *correctly*, feeling that the text had adjusted itself to my deficiencies and made itself manifest to my flawed eyes. Why did I not consign it to the flames then and there? I could have; the book held no control over me at that time. Or perhaps it did; perhaps I could never have destroyed it at all.

I know not how long I read last night. I remember none of it; I only remember awakening, hours later, still at my desk, the *Balremesh* opened to blank pages beneath me. I know I slept but fitfully, my dreaming filled with confined, dark spaces and small, dangerous things, hidden carefully in corners, which skittered away when looked for. I leafed through the book again to discover the pages *entirely empty*. The leaves of the book remained mottled, stained with age and other nameless substances, but not a single one now bore any writing in any language.

I remembered but a single phrase, rendered in an alien tongue yet somehow perfectly understandable. *Baal-Ramash y'gthul khatevish paan m'qthakk*. Welcome, revealer, Baal-Ramash, scourge of sin. I remember it as clearly as my own name; as clearly as my mother's face.

I am to open the door. I am to be the revealer of Baal-Ramash. *Baal-Ramash y'gthul khatevish paan m'qthakk*. But I must not. I must not open the door!

But I outpace myself. There is more of the tale yet to be told, before the door.

I closed the book and abandoned my writing-desk, intending to leave the foul thing and my library behind for a time. And then, somehow, suddenly, I found myself seated again, the book opened, the pages as stubbornly blank as before.

I tried again. I made it as far as the exit to the hallway. My hand reached for the door handle... and *stopped*. The book. Was the book closed, as it should be? I returned to my desk and closed the book. The insectoid creatures on the spine seemed more numerous and more malevolent than ever, and seemed to stare at me. I again turned to leave.

The book slid from my writing-desk, landed on its

back, open again.

But, this time, the book once again bore an inscription. Written in a bold, broad hand that seemed scorched into the paper, in a single line spread across both of the pages, that same arcane phrase that had burned itself into my memory: *Baal-Ramash y'gthul khatevish paan m'qthakk.* Welcome, revealer, Baal-Ramash, scourge of sin. And below, a woodcut drawing of thousands upon thousands of specimens of the degenerate, mutated horde.

It was then that the *sounds* began.

At first, they were subtle, whispers and moans hovering just above the threshold of what my ears could detect; always *behind* me, concealed by one of the shelves of my library or in some shadowed place the fire's light left untouched. Soon enough they grew to include other sounds; clattering in the walls and the floor, and the mad scramblings of dozens of diminutive invaders that sight and touch would or could not reveal. At times I nearly saw them—always, always in the corners of the room, or the dark angles between bookshelves. And always they disappeared as I drew closer.

I do not know when the door appeared.

It may be that it has always been there. It may be that it revealed itself when I first opened the *Balremesh*, or that the my night of unremembered reading somehow summoned it. It is there now, however—an ornate, stone door, with the same plate on its face as the cover of the book, and the same word: *Balremesh.*

It floats in the air, just before my fireplace, in the same spot where I first discovered the accursed book itself. But it *cannot.* It floats in the air without stand or hanging-wire as if perfectly natural. But such a thing *cannot be.* There is a handle. I know in my soul that the door is not locked, that I need only to reach out and take the handle and the door will open. But how, and to what?

I know that I am to open the door. The book *wants* me to open the door. It *demands* that I obey it. The sounds grow louder; the creatures no longer take such care to keep from my sight. *Baal-Ramash y'gthul khatevish paan m'qthakk.* Welcome, revealer, Baal-Ramash, scourge of sin.

In truth it can make no difference. I do not believe in magic, or spectral doors, or the strange creatures that emerge from blank books in the dead of night. None of this can be true. I am surely dreaming, and I will awaken in my bed or, perhaps, in my reading-chair in front of the fireplace.

I know that I am to open the door, and I know that I *must not* open the door.

I must not.

I must not open the door.

But I will.

Microfictions: Introduction

I spent a few months writing a bunch of 100-word stories in response to a photo prompt, and I liked a lot of them, enough to go ahead and include them here. Unfortunately, my attempts to locate and gain permission from the photographers to use their images were 100% unsuccessful. So here's how this section works: a brief description of the picture, and then the story. I hope your imagination can do the job for you.

Stonesrage Rock

A sandy beach. In the distance, a sheer, stony cliff. In the foreground, a single building.

"It's closer," the old man said. "Every year, an inch or two. The road splits. They fix it. But every year, it comes for us."

"You're loony, old man," I said. "That's a chunk of rock. It's pretty, that's all. It's not *coming*."

He smiled, his one good eye staring balefully at me. "The titans. The ancient ones of the earth, the *galevhdür*, they wait. And they watch. And when they come, they are inexorable. We anger the earth, child, at our peril. And it comes for us."

I walked away to his mocking laughter.

"You'll see, lad. You'll see."

Move to the Country! It'll be Great!

A straight, double-row of bulrushes in a marsh points directly at a home across a lake.

"Well, there's your problem." The old man spat, then crossed himself. "Faerie road, out there in the marshes. Pointed to your house."

I blinked. Twice. "What?"

"Aye. Brings the old ones out, it will. The sounds, the bangs, the cracks, the bugs. None of it the house. Their doing. All of it."

He leaned toward me. "I know one who could fix it. But not a carpenter. An exterminator."

Okay. "What's his name?"

"Don't worry about that, now," he said. "Just ... well, sometimes they're angry when their roads are

broken. Consider moving. Might be easier."
Suddenly I *really* missed Chicago.

Flight

A dozen or so people, in line to board a bus.

"This ain't gonna work," VJ grumped.

"Shuddup," I said. "He's not gonna find us."

"You were just on your phone," VJ said. "Bam. Signal everywhere. Tied straight to you. You turn off the GPS yet?"

"Dunno how," I said.

"Just turn the damn thing off."

I did. I'd ditch the electronics a town over, switch to burners. No updates anywhere. Radio silence. It'd be okay. Until I needed money, and used a card.

"You ever robbed anybody?" I asked. At least stolen money was clean.

"Just the once," VJ said. "I'll let you know if we get away with it."

Black House

A gated home in the French countryside. On the gate, a hand-painted sign reading "Chateau du Sable."

"Doesn't that mean 'Black House'?"

"Probably."

"It's *beige*."

"Maybe it means the *mold*," Pierce said, kicking a rock. "I don't know who named it. How long we gonna wait here?"

"Until he comes out," Karen said. "Dude has my lighter. I want it back."

"You serious?" Pierce said. "We're stalking a celebrity over a *lighter*."

"That and he's gonna marry me," she said.

"No."

"Yes."

"*No*. We're *leaving*." He grabbed her hand.

The knife came out, pointed at his crotch.

"'Kay." He backed off. "We wait."

Hopefully the gendarmerie had taken his call seriously. She got like this sometimes.

Luther M. Siler

Resolution

A private jet, outdoors.

It was a perfect day. The sky the deepest blue it could be, cloudless, the sun warming the tarmac just enough to make the day pleasant and not chilly.

I looked at *Morgan*. I'd named her after my one-and-only; I'd lost her namesake a few years back, but I still had the jet. Hadn't flown in a while. Wouldn't again, after today.

There was probably a cure, somewhere. I didn't need it. I needed to fly again, before they said I couldn't. And when I decided it was time...

...well, the Pacific was right there.

123

Please Do Not Touch

A wire, buried at both ends in rocky red sand.

"Don't touch it. It could be live."

"Live? Live how? What's it attached to?"

We looked around. There was nothing electrical for miles in any direction. Millions of them, if you didn't count our ship. And this cut, half-buried wire *definitely* didn't run to our ship.

"I'm gonna pull on it," Tyreena said.

"Are you nuts? It could–"

"Could *what?*" she interrupted. "This rock's *lifeless*. And someone's, what, running power to the bathrooms? It fell off our ship. Had to. I'm pulling."

A moment later, a flash and a sizzle, and the population of Galeb-IV was one fewer.

Compromise

A glass jar, full of miscellaneous batteries.

"Here you go."

Holtzman groaned. "What the hell is that?"

"You said you needed a battery. This is what we have."

This is the worst mad scientist lab of all time, Holtzman thought.

"You hired me to build a killbot. A *four-story tall* killbot. You were very specific about four stories. How do you expect me to power a four story killbot with AAA batteries?"

"I don't know," Gilbert sniffed. "*You're* the scientist. *You* figure it out."

Holtzman thought carefully for a few minutes.

"Fine. I can do *three* stories. But you're going to have to find me a nine-volt."

Priorities

A dark, foggy night, seen through a kitchen window over a full sink.

Eve watched the fog roll in over the lake and sighed. There was much to do before nightfall: secure the windows and doors, repour the salt at the threshold, and the garlic at the corners of the lot was probably rotten by now. She'd have to make sure they had enough candles, too; electric light drew more attention than fire. One might find a weak spot.

There was laundry, too, and the carpets needed vacuuming. At least the dishes were finished.

"Jim, can you take the trash out?" she asked, knowing the answer.

"In a minute, babe. The game's on."

Requests

A stained-glass window in a coffeeshop.

"You bring this to me," he said. "Why?"
"They say Papa Ortell's network is the best."
"Papa Ortell is an old fat man who wants to be alone with his croissant and coffee," he spat. "Not to be bothered by... *supplicants*." It was an insult.
"Jezka's been gone a week," I said. "Jezka owes me money. So Jezka owes *you* money."
He laughed, a short, brutal sound with no mirth. "Jezka pays to find Jezka, eh? Clever. Now go away." He waved a hand. And his eyes glowed, ice blue.
I felt bad for the kid. But not much.

Going Native

An hourglass.

She pointed. "That's how long you've got. Make it worth it."

"It wasn't my fault–"

She cut him off. "Bzzt. Try another one."

"It wasn't me!"

"*Fifteen* seconds."

"I was captured by aliens and replaced by a Gerotrossian replicant who managed to ruin my life in the 24 hours he had between insertion and his PseudoSkin simulant dissolving and needing to return to the mothership. I'm actually a space cop from Betelgeuse 19."

An eyebrow lifted.

"You have my attention. That was at least entertaining. One more minute."

Galactic Sergeant Olin Cardswallock rubbed his forehead. Sometimes undercover on-planet work wasn't worth it.

Miami

A rotting, plastic office chair, nearly entirely submerged in swampy water.

"There."

"What is it?"

"Desk chair, maybe. Plastic shell. The metal might still be good."

The scavvies pulled the chair out of the muck and tore it apart, discarding foam and fabric and setting plastic and metal aside. There were whoops and hollers from both of them– the ball bearings in the wheels were intact, and a tension spring. Sealed, so the salt hadn't gotten them yet.

"What was this? Business district?"

"Maybe. Cheap chair; maybe from a house, before the Atlantic swallowed it."

"Think there's more?"

"We'll look for another ten. Haven't seen a sea snake yet. I'm getting nervous."

Memories

A stone stairwell, outdoors, cracked and overgrown.

"It was right here, I'm telling you."

"I can't believe we're doing this, we're gonna get in *trouble–*"

"Shut up," she said tenderly, and drew him in for a kiss. "The school closed two decades ago. Nobody's *watching*. We had a way bigger chance of getting caught the first time."

"The first time the punishment wouldn't have been *jail*," he said. "Or, like, our *kids* finding out."

"They'll think it's *cool*," she said. "I remember *you* talking *me* into this last time. Now c'mere. Remind me why it worked."

They embraced, the leaves skittering on the stairs the only sound.

Distrust

A woman's right shoe, lying in a sewer grate.

There was just one shoe, abandoned, halfway in the gutter. I picked it up, looked at it.

It was a nice shoe. I didn't know much about shoes but the leather felt soft and expensive and it looked carefully assembled. I wondered if it'd been made by a cobbler. I'd never met a cobbler, but I liked the word. I liked eating cobbler, too, but not the human kind.

I looked at the underside of the shoe.

LEFT, it said, in thick black marker writing.

It was a right shoe.

I put it back down and left it there.

The Mansion

An antique piano sits against a wall. The baseboards are exquisitely detailed.

"Is that a harpsichord?"

"Nah, it's an old piano. Don't touch it." Joe pointed at the DO NOT TOUCH sign displayed above the keys.

Ed looked closely. The piano was carefully dusted, but one key had some extra wear on it. He hit it a few times. Nothing happened.

"Do *not* touch that," the butler commanded. "That piece is not part of the auction."

"Whatever you say, Al," Ed said, tapping the broken key a few more times just for giggles.

Elsewhere in the mansion, unnoticed by anyone, the door to the cave silently slid open.

Luther M. Siler

The City of Lights

An entry to a subway station sits in an abandoned field, In the distance behind it, a glass building blazes with light.

"Too easy."

"This is the place. Through there. The City of Lights has a back door."

"It practically says TRAP on the front. It's too *easy*."

"Fine. You stay out here. Dark's coming."

Kchik yanked at the handle. The door screeched open, rust flaking off the hinges, breaking off dry stalks of dead grass. The dark inside was absolute.

"You don't enter the City of Lights by sneaking through the dark, Kchik. It's wrong."

He never hesitated. "I won't forget, Faa. Take care of the girls."

Kchik entered the dark. The door fell closed. Faa waited.

It never reopened.

Luther M. Siler

The Vigil

A mother and daughter, wearing white, sitting in a graveyard.

"It's been a year," the girl in white said. She picked at a scab on her knee.

"That's right," the woman in white answered. "Tomorrow, we learn."

"Do we really have to stay up all night?"

"He was your father," the woman answered. "For your father, we wait all night."

"And if he rises?"

"If he rises with gladness, we welcome him. If he does not rise, we leave him."

"And if he rises without gladness?"

"Then we shall see," she answered. The ceremonial knife dug at her back. She would have to decide swiftly who it was for.

Thank You

...for reading *Balremesh and Other Stories*. If you enjoyed reading it, please consider leaving a review at Amazon.com, Goodreads, or any other book review site of your choice. Reviews are essential to gaining publicity for independently published books, and your thoughts are always welcome.

About the Author

Luther M. Siler was born in 1976 and currently resides in northern Indiana. Sharing his house with him are his wife, son and an assortment of pets. He has a job, but it's not as interesting as it used to be and it's probably different now anyway.

His other works include three books in the *Benevolence Archives* series, the near-future *Skylights* series, and a nonfiction book about teaching called *Searching for Malumba*.

You can follow Luther at his blog at http://www.infinitefreetime.com, or on Twitter at @nfinitefreetime.

Also by Luther M. Siler

THE BENEVOLENCE ARCHIVES, VOL. 1:

Troll evictions! Dwarf pirates! Daring rescues! Angry gods! Impossible technology! Oversized bars! Pissed-off ogres! Disrespectful spaceships! All this and a mild disregard for proper wound treatment!

THE BENEVOLENCE ARCHIVES, VOL. 1 is a novella-length collection of six short stories set in a

Balremesh and other stories

common universe. Combining elements of space opera-style science fiction and high fantasy, THE BENEVOLENCE ARCHIVES tell the adventures of Brazel, Rhundi, and Grond, a gnome/halfogre team of smugglers.

THE PLANET IT'S FARTHEST FROM: A simple job in a saloon goes poorly for Brazel.

THE CLOSET: Brazel and Grond are hired to teach someone why gambling can be a bad idea.

YANK: Dwarven pirates. 'Nuff said.

REMEMBER: Brazel and Grond are hired by one of the galaxy's most powerful people for a suspiciously easy job.

THE CONTRACT: Rhundi tries to get through a simple business negotiation without anyone being shot.

THE SIGIL: Brazel and Grond encounter something horrifying on a frozen rock in the middle of nowhere.

Luther M. Siler

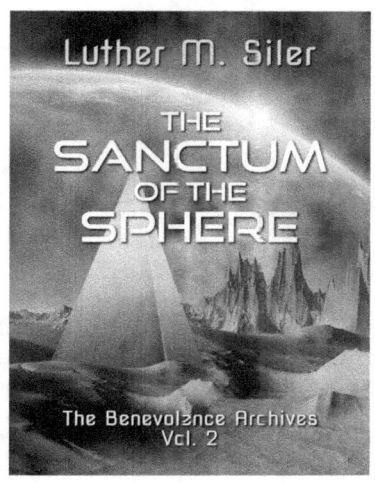

THE BENEVOLENCE ARCHIVES, VOL. 2: THE SANCTUM OF THE SPHERE

"Go rob that train." Nice, normal. An everyday heist.

But nothing is ever normal for Brazel, Grond and Rhundi.

A simple act of motorized larceny quickly explodes into a galaxy-spanning adventure for the two thieves. Blade-wielding elves, a fast-moving global war, a secret outlaw space city, incomprehensible insectoids and one impossibly lucky human are just the start of their problems. And that's before they learn that someone from Grond's past has gotten the Benevolence involved...

Balremesh and other stories

What is happening on the ogrespace moon Khkk?

Who are the Noble Opposition?

And what is the secret of THE SANCTUM OF THE SPHERE?

SKYLIGHTS

August 15, 2022: the *Tycho*, the most advanced interplanetary craft ever designed by the human race, launches from Earth on an expedition to Mars. The *Tycho* carries four passengers, soon to be the most famous people in human history.

February 19, 2023: The *Tycho* loses all communication with Earth while orbiting Mars. After weeks of determined attempts to reestablish contact, the

Tycho is declared lost.

2027: Journalist Gabriel Southern receives a message from a mysterious caller: "Mars." Ezekiel ben Zahav isn't talking, but he wants Southern to accompany him for something— and he's dangling enough money under his nose to make any amount of hardship worth it.

SKYLIGHTS is the story of the second human expedition to Mars. Their mission: to find out what happened to the first.

Read on for an excerpt: the prologue to SKYLIGHTS.

Flashbulb memory, they call it. It's when you remember exactly where you were when you first discovered something or saw something happen.

If you're younger than me, which a lot of you probably are, then your first flashbulb memory is probably related to terrorism somehow. Anybody in, say, their early thirties or older probably remembers exactly where they were on September 11, 2001. A little younger than that and your first flashbulb memory is probably one of the bombings in Chicago in 2018.

I was six years old when the space shuttle *Challenger* exploded. It was January 29, 1986, at exactly eleven thirty-nine in the morning. I was in first grade. For some reason— I could look this up if I wanted, I suppose, but my first-grade self didn't know, so I'm not going to bother— NASA had decided that it would be great if they put a schoolteacher on the Space Shuttle. Her name was Christa McAuliffe, and she'd been a middle school teacher, her students not a lot older than I was at the time.

There was a ton of publicity about her presence on the shuttle. Come to think of it, that might have been the reason that NASA put her there in the first place. Every single kid in my school was watching the flight launch on television. The *Challenger* took off, and we all clapped. Seventy-three seconds later, an O-ring failed on the shuttle's right Solid Rocket Booster. There was a little puff of smoke from the side of the ship.

Some of us were still clapping.

I remember noticing it and wondering, for the split second that I had, what had happened. And then the *Challenger,* with me and millions of other people around the country watching, silently blew apart. There were a few seconds of shocked silence in the room, and then every kid in the class— every one in the building, probably— started crying at once.

You know what? Writing that just now, I wondered what my teacher must have done afterwards. I can't even remember her name. I can remember the wood surface on my desk, because I dug my fingers into it so hard that day that they scratched it and I got splinters. I can remember the wood-grain on the television set they had us watching. I can remember being surprised that Rachel Douglas, the biggest butthead in the entire first grade, was crying as hard as I was. But I can't remember a

single thing that our teacher did to try and bring
everybody back to sanity after watching that happen.
That's how flashbulb memories work; you'll remember
the event itself forever, but that doesn't mean you'll
remember anything else that happened around it.

Seventeen years and two days later, it happened again.
This time, it was the shuttle *Columbia*, and I was twenty-
four and no longer sitting in a classroom. In fact, when
the *Columbia* was falling apart in the morning sky over
Texas, I was stuck in traffic and late to work. I found out
about it about ten minutes after I got in, when the smarmy
dope from the office next door made some sort of
comment about it to me. We had the Internet by then—
yes, there was Internet back then, although I think we
might have still been calling it the World Wide Web—
and I saw the entire thing on CNN's Web site. This time
there weren't any tears, just a dull sort of ache in the pit
of my stomach. I spent the rest of the day on the
computer, chasing down eyewitness reports and trying to
devour whatever little bits of actual news managed to
leak out. It was funny; I hadn't spent much time thinking
about space flight since the first grade, but suddenly the
families of the men and women on that shuttle were all I
could think about.

I was working for the *Indianapolis Star* at the time,
splitting my time between a biweekly column in the
science section and general reporting on local news for
the rest of the paper. It was a good job; I was happy

enough, and making enough money, but I wanted something different from my life.

I decided to write a book.

A year later, I'd completed *Nothing to Bury: the Martyrs of the Space Race*, a look at the lives of the astronauts who had died on the *Challenger* and the *Columbia*, as well as a host of other lives lost in the pursuit of space, and a look at the culture of NASA in between the two disasters. I was pretty proud of it as a piece of work; I wasn't expecting it to necessarily sell well to the general public, but it was a good piece of writing. It did better than I'd expected, enough that I've been able to be comfortable with freelance writing since then. I'm still working for news sites and some of the few print papers that are left, mind you, but I can pick my own assignments and do my own reporting now as opposed to having people assign my projects.

You know where this is going, don't you? I imagine you do.

On August 15, 2022, after years of technical and political delays, the space shuttle *Tycho*, carrying four astronauts, launched on a six-month journey to Mars. They were to remain in orbit around Mars for thirty days, during which they would land on the planet's surface for the first time in human history, then to return to Earth. The run-up to the launch was the biggest public relations bonanza NASA had ever seen. Everything just *stopped* the day the *Tycho* launched. It was just like it had been for the *Challenger,* only times a hundred. They just weren't as good at hype in the eighties, I guess.

I was watching at home, with a couple of friends— I actually had a little party for the launch. I didn't realize how tense I was until I looked at my hands afterwards. There were furrows in my palms from my fingernails. Then the shuttle took off, soaring into a perfectly blue sky, and I held my breath for a few moments.

The launch went off without a hitch, though, and pictures of the *Tycho* blanketed every website and print doc on the planet over the next few days. For the next six months, everyone was obsessed with Mars. The astronauts provided regular updates on what they were doing. You could get daily blink messages from them if you wanted to, and progress along their flight path was updated live on a map running at the top of CNN.com for the entire duration of the trip. Those six months, I'm convinced, inspired a whole generation of new astronauts, astrophysicists, and pilots. I've never in my life seen America more excited about science. It was amazing.

And then, on February 19th, 2023, when the long voyage was finally over, we... well, we don't actually know what happened. The *Tycho* was supposed to aerobrake into orbit around Mars, stay in orbit for a day or two, and then the astronauts were going to leave the ship to descend to the planet's surface in a lander. They were going to stay on the surface for two weeks or so, doing experiments, exploring the Martian surface, and making history.

There wasn't anything resembling photo evidence, not good evidence at least— NASA had been sending a steady diet of pictures and video from cameras affixed to the outside of the *Tycho* for months, but they failed at the same time as the audio feed. But we were getting audio beamed back from inside the cabin. Right up until the point where the flight commander, a decorated Marine pilot by the name of Alondra Gallegos, spoke the last words that the *Tycho* sent back to Earth.

"Is that..." was all she said.

After that, nothing. No sound, no signals, no big explosion to be played on the news over and over again. Just nothing at all, and what started off as mild concern slowly morphed, over the next few days, weeks, months, into the certainty that, somehow, the ship had been lost. There was hope for a while that there had just been some sort of global communications failure, that the *Tycho* was still out there but had lost the ability to talk to us. Sadly, those hopes didn't make much sense in reality— the *Tycho's* communication capabilities were among the simplest systems on the ship, something a talented twelve-year-old would have been able to repair, *and* there was a redundant backup system. Anything catastrophic enough to have completely crippled the ship's ability to talk would have caused fatal damage to the rest of the ship as well. We just couldn't figure out what.

Conventional wisdom eventually decided there had been some sort of asteroid or meteorite impact, something like that.

There was no flashbulb moment for the *Tycho*. The families of the four people lost on that mission— Alondra Gallegos, Harrison Brown, Kassius Newsome, and Ai-Li Wu— will never be able to move on. Many of them are convinced that their family members are still out there somewhere. There was no national mourning like there was for the *Challenger* and the *Columbia*. It was as if, after three high-profile ship losses, this time the country just wanted to forget about it.

I got a few calls for interviews after the *Tycho* lost contact, and a few more a few months later, once NASA officially stopped trying to reestablish contact with the ship. I turned them all down, though; I didn't want to base any more of my career on profiting from the deaths of people more heroic and important than I was. I didn't want to write about space any more.

Little did I know.

www.ingramcontent.com/pod-product-compliance
Lightning Source LLC
Chambersburg PA
CBHW060822120626
46557CB00001B/326